"What sort of work do you do, Mr. Anders?"

"I'm in the process of...changing gears." The sardonic lift of his eyebrow telegraphed his disdain. "I'll let you know." Whistling to his dog, he turned on his heel.

Megan watched him go, taking in his almost military stride and the rigid set of his shoulders.

She'd come here hoping to find a solid lead that would finally tie the assaults and murders to a single suspect. Beyond just that folder of receipts, a gut-deep feeling told her that he wasn't the one she was looking for.

But there was something else about him that wasn't quite right—and she was definitely going to find out what Scott Anders was hiding.

Books by Roxanne Rustand

Love Inspired Suspense

Hard Evidence
Vendetta
Wildfire
Deadly Competition
**Final Exposure*
**Fatal Burn*
**End Game*

*Snow Canyon Ranch
**Big Sky Secrets

ROXANNE RUSTAND

lives in the country with her husband and a menagerie of pets, many of whom find their way into her books. If not at her part-time day job as a registered dietitian, writing at home in her jammies, or spending time with family, you'll probably find her out in the barn with the horses or with her nose in a book.

This is her twenty-third novel, and is the third book in the Big Sky Secrets series. Her first manuscript won a Romance Writers of America Golden Heart Award, and her second manuscript was a Golden Heart Award finalist. Since then, she has been an *RT Book Reviews* Career Achievement Award nominee in 2005, and won the magazine's award for Best Superromance of 2006.

She loves to hear from readers! Her snail-mail address is P.O. Box 2550, Cedar Rapids, Iowa 52406-2550. You can also find her at www.roxannerustand.com, www.shoutlife.com/roxannerustand.com, or at her blog, where readers and writers talk about their pets, http://roxannerustand.blogspot.com/.

END GAME

ROXANNE RUSTAND

Published by Steeple Hill Books™

STEEPLE HILL BOOKS

Recycling programs for this product may not exist in your area.

ISBN-13: 978-0-373-67417-6

END GAME

This edition published by arrangement with Steeple Hill Books.

www.SteepleHill.com

Printed in U.S.A.

Send forth your light and your truth, let them guide me; let me bring peace to your holy mountain, to the place where you dwell.

—*Psalms* 43:3

Don't worry about anything. Instead, pray about everything. Tell God what you need, and thank him for all he has done. If you do this, you will experience God's peace, which is far more wonderful than the human mind can understand. His peace will guard your hearts and minds as you live in Jesus Christ.

—*Philippians* 4:6–7

With many thanks to Kylie Brant and
Cindy Gerard for the fun, the friendship
and our plotting weekends—and always,
to Dani and Ben with love!

ONE

"I won't stop until I find this guy, Anna." Seeing the raw pain in her friend's eyes, Megan Peters took a deep breath and forced back the memories threatening to swamp her. "I promise."

"How?" Anna lashed out, pulling her hands away from Megan's. "I didn't see his face. I don't know who it was, and neither did the other woman who got away. And the two *dead* girls won't be talking."

The bitterness in Anna's voice stung Megan as if she'd been slapped. "No. But the DNA—"

"Hasn't matched anyone in the system so far, and probably never will, right? This guy will never be caught."

"But it does connect the crimes, so when we get him, we'll be able to send him away for good. There'll be a time when someone picks up on a clue. Someone else who escapes."

They both fell silent, Megan's words a chilling reminder of the two women who had been raped and murdered within the past six months. If a group of noisy hikers hadn't come by and scared off her attacker, Anna might have been number three.

"We're doing our best," Megan added quietly. "And we *will* get him."

It wasn't an idle promise, and Megan could only hope Anna believed it. The younger woman had been a county 911 dispatcher for five years before resigning last winter, and she'd seen Megan in action. She also knew why this case mattered to Megan so much.

Anna turned away to brace her hands on the windowsill of the tiny Marshall County sheriff's office. "But until he's caught, he'll continue to prey on women, and that could go on for the next decade." Her voice rose. "I *know* how few deputies work this county, remember? Not enough. And it's huge. He could hide up in some remote cabin in the mountains and never be found."

Megan waited a few moments for her to

calm down. "Or he could be someone we see every day in town, and he could start making mistakes. If there's ever anything you can remember, call me, day or night. His shoes. Something in his voice. A gesture—"

Anna spun around, her face pale, a hand at the jagged, healing wound at the base of her neck. The bandages and sutures were gone now, leaving gnarled, dark pink flesh that would become a fainter scar in time. But Megan knew the real wounds—the emotional trauma and deep fear—were far worse, and might never fully heal.

"I came in once more because you asked me to, but please don't ask me again. It was dark. He didn't speak. Living through it all again and again is more than I can bear."

"I understand." At the anguish twisting Anna's lovely features, Megan felt a corner of her heart tear. "I'm more sorry than I could ever say, about everything you've been through."

Anna's mouth lifted in a sad smile. "I know you're trying. Look, I—I need to get back home. Lance has to leave for work at three, and I have to take care of Jeremy."

Megan watched her old friend zip up her heavy jacket, slip out the front door and limp down the sidewalk to the station wagon parked close by. At the driver's side Anna cast a swift, uneasy glance in both directions, then she slid behind the wheel.

Still in off-season for a few more weeks, until the end of May, when the mountain passes were more likely to be clear of snow, the town of Copper Cliff and the surrounding rural areas claimed less than four thousand year-round residents. Only a few of them were on Main Street now. Yet Megan had no doubt that Anna had hit the locks the second she got into her car.

A routine most of the local women now followed without fail day or night…in a town where no one had ever locked their doors until a killer had slipped into their midst.

"Any luck?"

At the sound of heavy footsteps and the scent of Old Spice aftershave behind her, she turned to face Hal Porter, the sheriff. She shook her head. "I was hoping she'd had time to sift through what happened. There just has to be something she can tell us."

"Unless she's too terrified to speak up."

"I can understand that with the other woman who escaped after being assaulted. But given Anna's years as a dispatcher, I thought there'd be a better chance that she could give us *something* to work with." Megan slashed a hand in the air. "I can't believe a guy could attack someone and never say a single word."

"I agree."

She lifted her eyes to meet Hal's weary gaze. "But whatever the guy said was so vicious, so threatening, she's afraid to talk. What kind of animal *is* he?"

"We'll find him. It's just gonna take time." Hal shook his head slowly as he turned back to his office, his decades of law enforcement clearly weighing more heavily on his shoulders with every passing month.

He didn't have to say it—she'd noticed the faraway look in his eyes and knew he was contemplating retirement. His wife, Greta, had been fighting cancer for a long time, and had recently taken early retirement from the local high school. He probably longed to spend his days with her…for whatever time she had left.

But he'd never been a man who'd walk away from trouble, or one who could leave a job undone. And no matter what called to him in his personal life, she knew he wanted to retire with this case closed, or he'd feel as if he'd failed.

Hal paused at his desk. "Go home, Megan. I mean it. You've been here well over your twelve hours already."

"It's still not enough." But when he folded his arms across his chest and gave her his trademark implacable stare, she checked her service belt, pulled the patrol car keys from her pocket and headed for the back door.

Going home without answers meant another day the killer roamed free, and the thought rankled.

Even after nine years as a county deputy known for being tough and in control, there was one kind of situation that still sent secret waves of nausea and anxiety through Megan's gut. And this time, yet another good friend had been a victim.

Men who preyed on women—whether domestic bullies or the animal now loose in Marshall County—had been a personal vendetta of hers since the day she'd gone into law enforcement, and that would continue until the day she took off her badge.

For the sake of all the women in the county—especially Anna, and Greta, a sweet, devoted woman who deserved more time with her husband before she died, Megan was going to make sure this case was solved.

And *soon*.

Scott Anders nodded at the clerk's farewell, gathered up his four canvas grocery bags and headed out to his truck.

From the day he'd moved to Montana, he'd been startled by the overt interest of the shop-keepers in Copper Cliff, who all seemed to know his name and even where he'd bought property up in the hills, as though through some sort of small-town osmosis.

The gum-chewing, fortysomething gal at the cash register of Roy's Grocery apparently counted him as an old friend, updating him on her teenagers, mother and husband, Erwin, every time Scott came in for supplies. At the tiny local drug store, Ralph, the elderly druggist, regaled him with tales of his grandchildren.

After a lifetime of anonymity in Chicago, the unexpected attention of everyone, from the guy at the feed mill to the gas station attendant, had initially set off alarms in his head; born of the instinctive wariness that had kept him safe on the streets for fifteen long years.

Now, he knew that the collective friendliness was something extended to all year-round residents, because there were just so few of them around. Though after running a gauntlet of shopkeepers during his monthly trips into town, Scott invariably heaved a sigh of relief when he could finally head back up into the foothills.

Jasper, his black lab, stirred on the front seat of the truck and hung his head out the passenger window to stare at the coffee shop across the street when Scott climbed behind the wheel.

Scott sighed. "We really oughta get back home."

Jasper looked at him again and whined, his

sorrowful expression speaking louder than any words.

From experience, Scott knew that if he didn't make the required trip across the street, the old dog would avoid meeting his eyes for the rest of the day, and the sulk could even stretch into tomorrow.

He reached over and gave Jasper a rub behind the ears. "You are *so* spoiled. Wait here, then. Fifteen minutes, tops."

Locking the door behind him, he strode over to Hannah's Pastries 'n' More and stepped inside. The place was done up in a profusion of red and white—frilly curtains and such meant to attract summer tourists. Even so, there were a couple of grizzled ranchers sitting at one of the tables, and a few more cowboys were at the far end of the long soda fountain, cradling mugs of the best coffee in town.

A woman sat alone on the swivel stool closest to the cash register, deep in conversation with Sue Ann, the day shift waitress. Her long auburn hair was caught up in a ponytail pulled through the back of a baseball cap, and from her faded denim jacket and jeans, he placed her as a daughter or wife of a local rancher.

A very pretty one, from what he could see from a brief glimpse of her face as she flicked a glance at him. He'd never seen her before, and he found himself wondering what color her eyes were, or if there was a ring on her hand.

An unfamiliar stirring somewhere in the region of his heart made him quickly rein in those foolish thoughts. The last thing he needed was any sort of personal complications, now or ever.

He settled at one of the empty spots halfway between her and the cowboys, and focused on the laminated, one-page menu tucked behind the napkin holder in front of him, though he already knew it by heart.

Sue Ann drifted down his way a minute later with a coffeepot in her hand. "Black, with Jasper's dog cookies to go?"

Even without turning toward her, he sensed the amusement of the woman sitting near the cash register. "Make the coffee to go, too."

"And here I thought I might interest you in some of the blackberry pie you like. You want a slice in a take-out container?" She winked at him, a hand propped on her hip. "Just think about that wonderful, flaky crust, and all of those sweet, sweet berries."

Scott nodded, then had second thoughts. "Maybe I'd better just stay here. Last time, we…had a little trouble with takeout."

Sue Ann laughed aloud. "Tell me your buddy didn't eat that pie."

"Down to the last blackberry."

Still grinning, she pulled a mug from the shelf beneath the counter, poured his coffee, then bustled back to the kitchen.

The other woman laughed as she turned to study him. "Trouble, eh?"

He angled a glance at her, then wished he hadn't.

Beneath the bill of her cap he could see flawless, creamy skin, touched by a faint blush of rose over her high cheekbones. Delicately arched brows. Sparkling green eyes that turned his heart upside down…until he caught her direct, frankly assessing gaze, and the way she'd positioned herself to keep her back to the wall.

The hair at the back of his neck prickled.

Pretty green eyes or not, he knew without

asking, exactly what she was…or had been. And the painful lessons were with him still.

He shook off his thoughts and gave her a neutral smile. "My dog Jasper loves the homemade dog cookies, but he loves pie even more. Last month, I got distracted by elk on the road. He managed to paw open the foam container and wolf down an entire slice before I could pull over and stop."

"I'll bet he was sorry later."

Her grin seemed to light up her face, transforming it from pretty to captivating, and he found himself smiling back at her. "The digestive complications weren't exactly pretty, but given a chance, I know he'd do it again."

"Sounds like my old dog."

He savored a slow sip of his coffee, nodding his thanks to the waitress when she slid an ample slice of pie and a paper bag of dog cookies in front of him.

She cocked her head as she searched his face. "I haven't seen you around town before. Visitor?"

"I moved here three or four months ago." At her upraised eyebrow, he added, "Up in the hills, above town."

Instant awareness dawned in her eyes. "You must've bought the Swansons' place. I remember hearing it sold last winter. Is your name..." She thought for a moment. "Anderson?"

"Anders. Scott Anders." He accepted her brief, firm handshake.

"Megan Peters." She cast a dismissive glance at her casual clothes. "County deputy, but you wouldn't guess it now. This is a rare day off."

Oh, I knew it, sweetheart. Cop or ex-military, before you even opened your mouth.

"So, how do you like it here?" She smiled, though he saw more than just casual curiosity lurking in her eyes.

"Fine."

"What sort of work do you do?"

"I'm taking a few months off." He turned back to his pie for a final bite and pushed the half-eaten piece away. Settling his Stetson in place, he rose, dropped a ten on the counter and headed for the door. "See you around."

He could feel her studying him as he walked out.

She probably thought he was rude, but it didn't matter.

He kept to himself and planned to stay that way.

And even if the contrast of her appearance and her profession was an all too interesting mix, Deputy Megan Peters was the last person in Copper Cliff he'd want to know any better.

"Interesting," Megan muttered under her breath as she watched Scott leave. "Was there a fire, or was it just me?"

Sue Ann moved down the counter to clear away his plate and coffee mug. "Neither, I'd guess. Actually, that's the most I've ever heard him say."

"How can he not have a job? Property around here doesn't come cheap."

The waitress shrugged. "He's only been in town a couple times that I know of, and he doesn't talk much. Maybe he's just another one of those rich dudes buying up property in the area." She flashed a quick smile at Megan. "He's a real good-looking guy, though…so I did ask around. No one else seems to know anything about him, either."

"He doesn't dress like some rich wannabe cowboy. Is he single?"

"Far as I know—unless he keeps the missus at home when he comes in for supplies."

If Sue Ann didn't have the information, probably no one did. Hannah's Pastries was the hub for all the news and gossip in the area. "Where's he from?"

Sue Ann shrugged. "No idea. I get the feeling he doesn't like a lot of questions…though he does seem like a nice enough guy. He sure loves that dog of his."

"What about the Swansons—are they still around?"

"I heard they rarely came up here anymore, so they finally decided to sell out and just spend more time at their beach house. They sold their property through an Internet listing, so they never met the buyer."

"I still can't believe I haven't run into him until now."

"No surprise, really, because he rarely comes to town."

Which seemed even more suspicious, the more Megan thought about it.

What sort of young guy moved up here and turned into a hermit, without visible means of support? Or got edgy and split the moment he found out he was talking to a deputy? He hadn't seemed particularly antisocial until then, so what was he hiding?

That flash of wariness in his eyes certainly hadn't been her imagination.

Megan's cell phone vibrated at her hip, and she reached for it. Hal's private number appeared on the screen. She headed for the privacy of the back of the café and answered it.

"Hey, Megan."

At the ragged note in his voice, her heart rate sped up. "What's up?"

"We...just got a 911 call." He drew in a slow breath. "Another body."

"Where?"

"Some hikers found it, a few yards from a trail going up to Granite Peak. Female, early thirties."

"You think it's the same guy?"

"I'm at the scene right now." He rapidly gave her directions. "And there's something here that you'll want to see."

TWO

Megan shivered, wishing she'd worn a heavier jacket. The lower elevations would be much warmer by now, but up here, heavy mounds of snow still covered the north-facing slopes and the shaded ground beneath dense stands of pine.

Though it probably wasn't the chilly weather that was making her shake. Even after years in law enforcement, approaching a murder scene triggered flashbacks of the night her childhood friend Laura had been murdered.

She'd never told anyone in the department. She hid the wrenching memories so well behind her mask of cool professionalism on the job, that many of the locals thought it eerie, how she felt so little emotion in the face of death.

But none of those people had ever followed her home. None could see into her heart.

And now, seeing Hal's haggard expression as he stood waiting for her on the trail ahead, that empty and aching place in her chest made it almost hard to breathe.

She stepped forward. The body, now covered by a plastic sheet, lay a few yards off the trail partially obscured by thick brush, the snowy surroundings as cool as a slab in a morgue.

"When the call came in, I took it myself." Hal lifted his clipboard and scanned his notes. "The hikers were two high school kids who saw the body from the trail. They were nearly hysterical when they called 911. They say they didn't approach the victim, so hopefully the scene wasn't contaminated."

"Was the body covered?"

"Only clothing, nothing else. And no attempt at burial, far as I can tell. That wouldn't have worked anyway—the surface is muddy, but the ground beneath is still frozen."

She nodded. "And the ground is awfully rocky—even in the summer, it would be tough. Maybe he figured there wouldn't be any people up here this early in the season. It wouldn't take long for scavengers to consume most of the evidence. Bears, coyotes, wolves—and in a few weeks, vegetation would hide the bones."

"True. And that makes me think the killer is a local, who knows the area well."

She crouched, pulled on a pair of vinyl gloves and slowly pulled back the edge of the tarp, dreading her inevitable, initial flash of shock and horror; hiding her emotions with perfect stillness. Anything less than pure professionalism was a sign of weakness she refused to show.

She murmured a silent prayer for the deceased as she surveyed the battered face, the deep, gaping laceration across the throat. The body was clothed only in a torn, designer label shirt that covered it from neck to midthigh, the gray flesh was streaked with mud and strewn with pine needles. Even so, she could see that the victim had once been a very attractive woman.

"Have you called the DCI?"

"They ought to be here any time now."

Megan studied the body, thankful for

a chance to check out the scene before the state crime investigation team showed up. "I'd guess she's been dead at least forty-eight hours, though these cold nights make it harder to tell. Given the position of the lividity markings, I'd say the body was moved at least eight hours after the time of death."

"Agreed." Hal gestured toward a faint path winding through the trees. "There's a rough fire road off in that direction, a good half mile away. Someone kicked debris over the trail, but you can still see some marks in the ground where the body was dragged over here."

"Whoever did it had to be strong. I'm guessing a fairly big and burly guy." She surveyed the rugged terrain. "Any footprints?"

"Nothing clear, but I didn't want to disturb anything. This isn't our usual act-of-passion or barroom brawl kind of death. Those aren't hard to sort out. But this one..." His voice trailed off and he shook his head. "The DCI investigators will go over this area inch by inch, and hopefully between them and their mobile lab, we can make more progress on finding our killer."

At that, she forced herself to rise and take a step back.

He sighed heavily. "I did lift her fingerprints, though. When I get back to the office I'll start checking missing person's reports. Her family's probably worried sick about her, wondering where she is."

"They've all been brunettes," Megan whispered. "Attractive. All in the same general age range. Slender. Married, or at least engaged. And there's an indentation on her ring finger."

"Just the things I wanted you to see. The similarities are striking." He pursed his lips. "The killer took her rings, just like he did with the other two. Yet none of those rings have turned up in any pawnshops so far…or on the major Internet auction sites. At least, far as we can tell."

"He's keeping trophies."

"He could be dismantling the rings for the stones—less chance of them being traced. Or he could be waiting to move them until things cool down."

Megan shook her head. "It's not about the money. Did you take a look at the earrings this one was still wearing? They look like eighteen karat, and that sure isn't a cheap knockoff watch on her wrist. The second victim still wore her diamond tennis bracelet."

He stared down at the black plastic sheet. "True."

"This has to be the same killer. The body positioning is identical. Faceup, fingers interlaced over the chest. Ankles crossed—as if it mattered that the body was tidy and modestly displayed after a brutal murder. None of these details have been leaked to the press. Once we have an ID on the body, we'll need to track her activities over the past few months and see if that's a match, too."

There were dozens of popular roadhouses in the county—old-west styled bars offering steaks and burgers, live country music and beer. All of the victims had frequented those places in the months before their attacks.

Hal lifted his gaze to meet hers and nodded, the quirk of his mouth conveying his approval of her assessment. "What else?"

"Timing. Full moon, every time—or as close as forensics can get for placing the time of death. If the papers pick up on that, I can just see the headlines…and that sort of notoriety and attention could fuel this guy's motivation." She leveled a look at him. "But I'm sure you have all this figured out, anyway. Why do I get the idea that you're testing me?"

His silent answer was evident in the deep lines of his face and the weariness in his eyes.

They'd had this conversation a dozen times. Her answer was always the same, but this time, she felt rising sympathy warring with her resolve. "You know I'm not interested."

"Once this case is over, I'm leaving. You're the right one for the job. You'd make a good sheriff."

"I belong in a patrol car, not behind a desk. I'd go *crazy* behind a desk."

"I'm not just at my desk. I'm out here, aren't I?"

"Whenever you can be." From somewhere in the distance came the faint sound of approaching vehicles at the bottom of the hill, and they both fell silent for a moment, listening. One of the engines sounded like a car, the other like a diesel truck—which could be the DCI's mobile lab unit. "But it's just not enough for me. Like this case—there's nothing I want more than to get this guy, if it takes every last minute, night and day. The politics and management you have to deal with would keep me from making a real difference out on the streets."

"You've already made a difference. Many times," he added gently. "Though you've already taken too many chances with this case. You need to learn to step back."

"I'd never jeopardize the safety of a fellow officer. You know that."

But last month she'd put a dark rinse in her hair, piled on some makeup, and had gone undercover in some of the roadhouses in parts of the county where she wasn't well-known. Places the victims had visited within a week of their deaths, just to see if anyone suspicious would approach her.

She'd rationalized those visits with the logic that she had the right to a taste of social life during her free time, and hadn't mentioned her off-duty ruse to Hal since he'd already denied her proposal to pursue an undercover operation.

His written reprimand was now a part of her file.

"I ran into a stranger at the café today. I'm going to run his name through the system, then go check him out."

"A tourist?"

"He bought the Swanson place. The place sold last November, yet he supposedly has only been here since some time in January. Interesting parallel with the killer's activities."

"Haven't met this new guy, either." Hal shrugged. "But it isn't surprising. Outsiders don't usually stay year-round unless they're into winter sports."

"True. He came in January, so maybe he's a skier—though there aren't any big resorts around here. He turned edgy when I mentioned being a deputy, and lit out of that café like a cougar after a lame deer."

Hal's gaze sharpened, locked on hers. "Be sure you have backup nearby when you go out there."

"I will." She suppressed a flash of frustration. Even after her nine years on the force, she still caught occasional hints of a faint, paternal tone in his voice. "But if it were Jim or Wes going out there, you wouldn't say that."

"If I was sending either one of them to

interview a suspect at an isolated place? It's *policy,* Megan."

"You can ride along if you want to."

He must've caught the edge in her own voice, because his mouth flattened to a grim line. "I get the feeling this case is way too personal for you, and it worries me. How many hours of your own time have you put in? Way, way too much."

"It's my job." She glanced down at the plastic tarp and couldn't quite suppress her inward shudder as a pervading sense of looming danger slid through her. "I don't want this killer to claim another victim."

"And I don't want to lose a good officer. You'll be off this case entirely if you don't watch your step."

The criminal records database yielded nothing on Scott Anders. Neither did the sex offender registry. The only hits Megan found were a couple of speeding tickets in Chicago from several years back, and as she pulled to a stop in front of his cabin, she wished once again that she'd nabbed his coffee cup at the café so she could run his prints through the national AFIS fingerprint database.

If Sue Ann hadn't abruptly turned to clear away his dishes, Megan would've done it…but she could only imagine the woman's questions and the potential for rumors, if she'd asked to *borrow* it for an hour or two.

These days, with *CSI* reruns scheduled almost nightly on television, Sue Ann would've latched on to the reason for her request in a split second.

After ten miles of nearly deserted two-lane highway, a turnoff led to five miles of gravel road that twisted up into the foothills. Here and there, pine forest gave way to glimpses to the west—sweeping panoramas of a deep valley, with a backdrop of the soaring peaks of the Rockies.

The lane leading to Anders's cabin had been even steeper, more narrow, the loose sand and rocks providing intermittent traction.

Now, Megan made a quick call to another deputy to let him know she'd arrived, and then she stood at the door of her patrol car and surveyed Anders's property. He must have had a great job, an inheritance or had won a lottery to buy a place like this one. Or maybe he'd found another less upstanding way to accumulate a great deal of cash.

The cabin itself was a sprawling, one-story log home with large windows facing the mountains. Behind it, several buildings were tucked among the pines. An unseen door slammed, and soon a black lab came loping around the side of the house, its tail wagging and tongue lolling.

"You must be the infamous Jasper," she said, laughing as the dog wound around her legs, its body wiggling with pure delight. "What a watchdog you are."

Anders followed a minute later, his businesslike stride and grim expression showing no sign of welcome. He gave the patrol car a disparaging glance, then took off his sunglasses and pinned her with a steely look. "Is there something I can do for you, *Officer?*"

Her second impression echoed her first.

He was tall—maybe six foot two, two-hundred pounds. Well muscled, without an obvious ounce of fat on him, and good-looking in a rough-hewn sort of way. A strong jaw darkened with a five o'clock shadow. Sweeping eyebrows. A shock of unruly, near-black hair tumbling over his forehead.

He looked liked someone who might model a Rolex or a black leather blazer on the pages of *GQ* magazine.

Handsome enough to attract a pretty woman.

Big enough to overpower her if she resisted his unwelcome advances.

In this isolated place, there'd be no one around to observe any suspicious activities. And he definitely didn't seem to appreciate the arrival of someone in uniform.

His dog ambled over to him and sat at his feet.

"Beautiful place you have here."

"It is."

"Great place to raise a family."

"I suppose it could be."

"You're here alone?"

"I like peace and quiet."

She glanced at the cabin, and the meadow surrounding it, where a few early wildflowers were peeking through the dried grass. "Will you be here year-round?"

"Yep. Why?"

"Most folks are just here seasonally, so if properties are going to be vacant, it's good for us to know. When did you say you moved in?"

His gaze sharpened on hers. "Are these questions leading anywhere in particular?"

"Out here, people tend to rely on each other—especially when there's trouble. It's good to meet new neighbors."

A corner of his mouth curled. "You're saying you're a neighbor?"

"Not exactly. But I work this part of the county, so I make it my business to get to know as many residents as I can." She tipped her head in a faint shrug. "And you left the café awfully fast."

He stood, silently waiting. She looked right back at him and smiled until he finally heaved a sigh. "I get the feeling that you've already checked me out, even before coming here. Maybe you can tell me what this is about, because otherwise I have nothing more to say."

She hesitated. He'd radiated a lazy sort of impatience before, but now she sensed his irritation. "There's been some intermittent trouble in the county, and I'm checking out possible leads."

"What kind of trouble?"

"The investigation is…ongoing. Were you in Montana during December? Just looking the place over, maybe?"

"No."

"What about when you bought the place?"

"All online. Look, Ms. Deputy, I do read the papers. I know about the two women who were killed." His expression was matter-of-fact, his voice cold. "I looked at this place last fall, bought it in November, and moved here the beginning of February. Hold on a minute."

He stalked back to the cabin and returned a few minutes later with a manila folder. "I know I don't have to answer your questions, and I don't have to show you this. But I just want to be left alone, and hope this will be the end of it." He handed her the folder. "I've got tollway, credit card and hotel receipts from my trip between Chicago and here. A receipt for the rental van. If this isn't enough, I can get copies of credit card statements that show transactions made in Chicago dated clear up through February 1."

Her heart sank as she thumbed through the folder and felt her chances at a quick resolution to the case slipping away. She handed it back to him. "I guess you're covered."

"I wasn't anywhere near here when those women were murdered. So unless you have something else, I think we're done with this conversation. Right?"

"What sort of work do you do, Mr. Anders?"

"I'm in the process of…changing gears." The sardonic lift of his eyebrow telegraphed his disdain. "I'll let you know."

Whistling to his dog, he turned on his heel.

She watched him go, taking in his almost military stride, and the rigid set of his shoulders.

She'd come here hoping to find a solid lead that would finally tie the assaults and murders to a single suspect. Beyond just that folder of receipts, a gut-deep feeling told her that he wasn't the one she was looking for.

But there was something else about him

that wasn't quite right—and she was definitely going to find out what Scott Anders was hiding.

THREE

The regular staff meeting in the sheriff's office fell on the second Monday of the month, which was usually a time for coffee, caramel rolls and camaraderie between the sheriff and the seven full-time deputies. Twelve-hour shifts, a budget too tight to hire extra personnel, and the county-wide area they all covered generally precluded the chance to gather at any other time.

Working so shorthanded, with three officers on leave, had kept them on edge for weeks. But today, with the murder investigation weighing heavily in everyone's minds, the mood was tense.

Megan fidgeted in her chair and studied the other deputies in the room, eager for Hal to wrap up the meeting so she could get back into her patrol car.

As if he'd read her mind, Jim Rigby caught her eye and canted his head in a subtle nod. Tall, fit and highly professional even after thirty years on the force, silver-haired Rigby was the deputy Megan most preferred to work with if she had a choice for a particular assignment.

Now, he glanced out the window in Hal's office, then turned to the others with a grim smile. "Mayor's coming. He doesn't look happy."

She smothered a laugh as Ewan Baker and Wes Dearborn simultaneously looked up at the clock, stood and—no surprise—edged toward the door. Short and hefty, with thinning brown hair, Wes was flat-out intimidated by the mayor's tendency for histrionics and avoided him at all cost. Ewan took considerable pride in his own intellect, and only tolerated the mayor if under duress.

"Guess we're done for the morning. Right, Sheriff?" Ewan muttered, smoothing a hand over his military-cut red hair. "I expect he wants to meet with just you anyhow, so we'd better get back to work."

He and Wes were out the back door within seconds after Hal nodded.

Mayor Taylor bustled in the front door and made a beeline for Hal's office without stopping at the front desk, a folder clutched to his narrow chest and his gaunt face a mask of worry. He ignored Megan and Jim, and marched forward to plant his hands on Hal's desk.

"It's been five days since that last body was found," he barked. "What's going on with this investigation? I need to know, Hal."

Megan rose to leave, but Hal motioned for her and Jim to stay. "You should see this," he said. "It's what you'll be hearing out in the county, from now on."

Taylor pulled a section of the newspaper from his folder and spread it out on Hal's desk with a flourish. "Look at these headlines and tell me what on earth we're going to do."

The bold headlines were clear, even from a distance and upside down. Full Moon Killer On The Loose. Megan exchanged glances with Jim and shook her head.

Some people fed on notoriety; the thrill of hitting the headlines and the sense of superiority gained from eluding the law spurring them on. Was that the kind of person they were dealing with? If so, the situation had taken a serious turn for the worse.

An image of Scott Anders slid into her thoughts.

There was nothing about him that suggested anything of the sort…but whether he'd been irritated or not by her visit, she'd only been doing her job.

The sheriff leaned back in his chair, his face an unhealthy shade of gray. "We can't stifle the press…much as I'd like to. But this is exactly what we'd hoped to avoid."

"You don't look too surprised," Taylor snapped.

"Clayton was in here yesterday, asking questions. I tried to convince him to avoid running this kind of headline, but he obviously didn't listen."

"Do you know what this is going to do to the area? Tourist season is just weeks away. Headlines like this will be picked up by the national news, and what will happen then?" His face ruddy, he took a deep breath. "We've already suffered thanks to gas prices and the economy over the last few years. Things were just starting to look up again, but some businesses can't handle another bad year. Hysteria over the presence of a deranged killer in this county is the last thing we need."

"We're doing all we can with the manpower and resources we have, Philip. This isn't New York or Los Angeles."

"But—"

"We're short-staffed at the best of times, as you well know. And until Dalton and Harrison come back from medical leave and Gustafson gets back from settling his dad's affairs, things are even worse."

"What about the DCI—don't they have any answers yet? They were here last Thursday, weren't they? That's four days!"

Hal tapped a stack of papers on his desk. "We got their preliminary report this morning."

"And?"

"We're doing all we can, but we don't know much more than we did before." Hal tipped forward and rested his forearms on the desk. "A missing persons report from Latimer County led us to the last victim's identity. Dee

Kirby. Jim spent the weekend interviewing her friends and family, and we know she visited the Halfway House Tavern—that rowdy bar on the south edge of Battle Lake. Dee was engaged, but still liked joining her old friends for a girls' night out whenever her fiancé worked late. She was there at least twice during the month before her death."

"And?"

"The last time they went, Dee's friends went off with guys they met there, leaving her to drive home alone. They feel terrible about it now, but at the time she assured them that she'd be fine. The bartenders remembered her from a photo. No one remembers her being flirtatious or wild, or remembers seeing her being harassed by anyone when she left."

"What about all the customers?"

"We're still working on the regulars, but it's impossible to find everyone. Cowboys come in on Saturday nights from remote ranches and pay cash, so there's no way to trace credit card records, and some of those boys are fairly transient. People come from all over the county for the music, but there are others who are just passing through."

"So you have *nothing* to go on?"

"No one we talked to remembers an altercation out in the parking lot that night, but it's dimly lit and the loud music would make it hard to hear, so that doesn't mean much," Jim said.

Hal nodded. "Anyone could have been lurking out by her car. Maybe someone even made a pass at her out there, then marked her as his next victim. Or secretly tailed her to find out where she lived."

"What about fingerprints? DNA, and all that?" Taylor sputtered. "Surely there must've been *something* out at the murder scene to go on."

"In a perfect world…or on TV," Megan said evenly. "But we don't believe she was murdered there, so there wouldn't be signs of struggle, and the DNA tests take a long time. The DCI did an extensive sweep of the area where the body was found, but didn't find anything—not even a clear footprint or tire track, which is hard to believe."

The mayor scowled. "And in the meantime, this killer is walking free, ready to strike again."

"We're dealing with someone who is smart. Skillful. Who *knows* how to avoid leaving clues. We know the other two murders and the two assaults are connected—the DNA evidence matched. Unfortunately, that DNA evidence didn't match anyone in the national database."

"And now, the level of tension in this county is going stratospheric, and you can't do anything about it."

"That's not true," Hal interjected. "This entire department is following up on every possible lead, day and night. This guy *will* slip up. Believe me."

The mayor's eyes narrowed. "I hear you had a good lead just last week…and you let him slip through your fingers."

Jim, Hal and Megan exchanged glances. "Now, who would that be?" Hal gave a short laugh. "Believe me, if we find this guy, he won't be getting away."

"Your deputy questioned him, right in the café." The mayor's face turned a deeper shade of red, his voice rising with every word. "I heard so, on good authority. It was a stranger, who's been in the area for the right amount of time. Surly, too. And he walked right out that door of the café without even a peep from the law. Do you honestly think Megan is capable—"

"*Sir.*" Through the open door of the office the receptionist's voice rose. "You can't just go barging in there. *Sir—*"

A man responded, his voice too low for Megan to catch the words, and a second later, a tall, dark figure filled Hal's doorway, silhouetted by the morning sun streaming in behind him. He radiated a commanding aura of power and an all too familiar air of impatience, from the wide set of his boots to the muscular arms folded across his broad chest. Scott Anders.

Megan stifled a groan. *Great timing.*

"Since I seem to be the topic of conversation, I thought I'd better join in," Anders growled, glancing dismissively at the others in the room, before settling his attention on her. "I thought we had this straightened out. Or did you come back here with an entirely different story?"

The mayor shrank back, his color draining.

Hal stood. "Now, see here, Mr.—"

"It's all right," Megan said quickly. "Scott Anders, this is Sheriff Hal Porter, Mayor Philip Taylor, and Deputy Jim Rigby. Scott is a new property owner up in the hills. He bought the Swanson place."

Anders's eyes didn't veer from her face. "I guess it's good that I came in about a dog license, or you might've had me behind bars before sundown."

"The mayor apparently heard some gossip down at the café." She glanced at the other men in the room. "After a very brief encounter at the café, I considered Mr. Anders to be a person of interest, so I went to his place to talk to him."

"You just *questioned* him?" Taylor shot back. "What does that prove?"

"He wasn't in Montana during the time frame of the first two murders. He has *proof*."

The mayor's gaze flicked between her and Scott, doubt creeping across his florid face. "What sort of proof?"

"Stacks of receipts from Chicago, and from his trip out here. Receipts that he can produce, to end this once and for all. Right, Mr. Anders?"

His shoulder jerked with impatience.

"Which could be falsified. They could've been...been from someone else," Taylor blustered. "Deputy Peters clearly isn't competent if—"

"Give it a rest," Hal broke in. "We'll take another look at his alibi, then consider it a done deal. I'm sure Deputy Peters was thorough and can handle this immediately. Right, Megan?"

A muscle along Anders's jaw jerked. Regret shone in his eyes as he slowly reached for the wallet in his back pocket, pulled out two cards, then flipped them onto Hal's desk. "Chicago. Call Pearson day or night. Ask him anything you want to know."

Hal studied them, his jaw slack, then he dropped the business card in his shirt pocket and handed back the identification card bearing an embossed gold shield. "You're a *cop?*"

"Was," Anders bit out. "Past tense."

Silence fell in the room, and Hal cleared his throat. "I'll make that call, and Megan will follow up on those pertinent receipts. Then I imagine we won't have to be bothering you again."

Out on the sidewalk twenty minutes later, Megan strode to her car, wondering if anyone could see smoke rising from her ears.

Big mystery, she fumed. And she'd ended up looking incredibly stupid for thinking he could be involved in murder and mayhem.

Then again…what was some underpaid Chicago cop doing out here, sitting on a valuable piece of property without a job? It didn't make sense.

Cops weren't perfect. Even out here, there'd been a pair of crooked officers in the department just before she was hired, and those two were still serving time.

"Hey."

Surprised, she spun around at the sound of Anders's voice and found him leaning against the door of a black Ford F-350 crew cab pickup, his arms folded across his chest and one booted ankle crossed over the other.

"Why didn't you tell me that you're a cop?"

He held up his hands in mock surrender. "I'm not any longer."

"You didn't think that information was pertinent when I stopped out at your place?"

"I didn't think I had to share my whole résumé. It's no longer a part of my life that I even want to think about."

"Then why did you tell everyone now?"

He shrugged. "They were questioning your ability. It seemed only fair."

She bit back a retort, realizing that he'd just tried to be kind. "Then what are you doing out here, now that you're in Montana?"

"Like I said back at my place, I'm changing gears."

"So, what's the big secret?"

He held her gaze for a moment, then looked away. "No secret intended."

In that brief moment of connection between them, a shiver of awareness danced across her skin. She took a step back. "Then tell me."

"Look, I've always been a writer of sorts, in my spare time, but I'm looking at trying to make it a career. As far as law enforcement is concerned, I'm on medical leave right now, but decided I'm not ever going back. End of story."

Given the ring of finality in his voice, he wasn't planning to elaborate, which only spurred her curiosity. "So how long were you a cop?"

Turning to open the door of his truck, he made a sound of impatience. "It doesn't matter. Look, the sheriff wants verification of my whereabouts. I'll drop off some photocopies of my receipts at his office in a day or so, when I can get back to town. And then we should be square."

"Hal figured that business card of yours was good testimony on who you are. Would that be true?"

He laughed, though there was a tone of bitterness in his voice. "Oh yeah, a badge guarantees I'm an upstanding citizen, all right."

"It sure didn't here, a decade back."

"Not anywhere." He slid behind the wheel and slammed the door shut, resting an elbow in the open window as he turned the key. The engine roared to life. "Cops go bad, too. They see more temptation than most. Kickbacks. Drugs and cash go missing between an arrest and the evidence room. A chance to send the kids to a private school can hinge on turning a blind eye. Who's to know? I've seen all that and more, and I've had enough."

There were shadows in his eyes that she couldn't quite read. Had he been personally involved, caught up in a chain of events he couldn't control? "I'm sorry."

"For what?"

"About whatever situation you left behind."

"It was nothing. Absolutely nothing." He looked in the rearview mirror, then threw the shift in reverse. "See you around."

He drove off without a backward glance.

FOUR

Scott leaned his arms on the top of the split rail corral and eyed the donkey's placid expression.

The single, long stemmed rose dangling from its mouth added a debonair flair completely contradicted by the animal's cockeyed left ear and ragged, 1970s shag carpet of a coat.

The corral fence was intact—all three rails solid. The two gates were still chained shut. The poor guy was dead lame and couldn't possibly jump, so how on earth had he managed to trample the roses up by the cabin and reappear in his corral with one clenched in his teeth?

Shaking his head, Scott laughed when the animal began methodically chewing, apparently oblivious to the sharp thorns on the stem. “Well, Attila, if you want it that bad, you deserve it, buddy. I’m just glad ole Mrs. Swanson isn’t here to see you stealing her roses.”

The absurdity of the situation hit him like a sucker punch to the gut as he turned for the cabin.

Six months ago he’d been working sixteen-hour days as a seasoned homicide detective. And now he was in the middle of nowhere. Living alone. He hadn’t seen another human being for five days, and he was talking to a *donkey.* Not that being alone was all that bad. Some of the alternatives were worse.

Like running into that cute little deputy, time after time—when the last thing he wanted was to feel that level of attraction ever again for a woman wearing a badge.

Or the situation with his ex-fiancée, who had pretty much cured him of any desire for commitment at any rate.

Just the fact that Olivia had broken their engagement would’ve stunned him, but her announcement that she’d eloped with her partner had been like acid on an open wound.

He’d immersed himself in his work after

that. Avoided the two of them whenever possible, maintained an air of cool detachment when he couldn't. As a beat cop, she didn't work out of the same part of the building, but there were chance encounters in stairwells and the parking lot…and then three months ago things had taken a far deadlier turn.

As he turned for the house, his cell phone vibrated at his belt.

Calls were rare these days, between the poor reception in the area and his efforts at complete isolation from his past, and he preferred it that way. He ignored the caller for a moment before unclipping the phone with a sigh of resignation. Whoever it was, it probably wasn't about anything good.

A glance at the screen confirmed his assumption. Bob. A retirement-age detective, he'd been one of the many in the department who had faded into the background when the accusations against Scott started surfacing. Apparently still uncomfortable with his spineless defection and trying to make amends, this was the second time he'd called.

"Yeah?"

"Hey." After an awkward pause, Bob cleared

his throat. "How's medical leave going? You doing okay?"

Rubbing the still-tender surgical scars on his shoulder, Scott forced himself to relax his grip on the phone. "Great."

"I…well, I thought you should know how things are going here." Another pause. "And again, I wanted to tell you that I'm real sorry. It shouldn't have happened. Not to a guy like you…"

Scott tuned him out.

One day he'd been trying to forget Olivia's romantic departure for a cocky young rookie cop whose ego was only exceeded by his bodybuilder brawn. The next—thanks to an anonymous tip—Scott had faced accusations about evidence that disappeared during a murder investigation.

Ten grand in unmarked bills and five kilos of prime White Widow, to be exact. Evidence that Scott had logged in himself, following procedure to the letter.

The dope disappeared, but the unexpected night deposit of ten grand into his checking account that followed, and the "stray" bullet that hit him a month later during the pursuit of a homicide suspect, had sure changed his life in a hurry.

He was on medical leave now, and had no intention of going back. He shook his head and returned to the present.

"The news isn't so good," Bob muttered.

Scott clenched his jaw. "It doesn't matter anymore, as far as I'm concerned. The Internal Affairs investigation cleared me and the last I heard, they'd hit a brick wall trying to determine who was responsible."

"A drug dealer was brought in last week." Bob made a sound of disgust. "Real upstanding citizen once he got arrested, if you know what I mean. He wanted to deal. Said you kept that stolen dope on ice, then offered it to him for half the street value."

Scott's heart took an extra hard thud. "Not possible. I'm here, remember? In Montana."

"People travel. You got witnesses, who can prove you've been out there nonstop?"

No one, other than Attila and Jasper, and neither of them could talk. "Has this guy been interrogated?"

A long silence stretched over the miles. "It won't be happening."

"But if the guy is accusing me of a felony—"

"He made bail. Less than twenty-four hours later, he turned up dead."

"What?"

"Looked like a professional job." Bob cleared his throat. "I know he was lying about you, trying to save his own skin. The chief thinks so, too. Just thought I'd mention that you might get a call about what you've been up to lately. There's been some talk about how convenient it was that this guy was iced right after offering testimony."

Scott mentally sorted through his past cases. Any one of the perps he'd put behind bars could've ordered a pal to exact revenge. Someone fresh out could've dwelled on it every hour he was behind bars. Executed a plan for retribution. "He have a name?"

"Mendez. Rico Mendez."

Scott flashed back to the murders of several gang members. Homicide—with Scott leading the case—had traced the crime to two men working under Mendez in south Chicago...and ultimately, that had led to one of the biggest drug busts on record for the department.

Those two were in the midst of appeals, but would undoubtedly end up on death row. Mendez, insulated by several levels of minions, hadn't been touched. Only now he was dead.

"The chief is still behind you, buddy…even with all the evidence against you. Just thought you should know."

"There *was* no real evidence." Reining in his rising frustration, Scott lifted his gaze to the towering mountains, now washed in soft amber early morning light. He considered his words carefully. "I know this case has been fuel for a lot of locker room gossip. But I kept a carbon copy of my log-in documentation in the evidence room. Joe was at the window and testified about seeing me."

"Though he didn't actually *examine* the contents of the packages."

"True. That was my one mistake. I should've stayed to make sure he did, but I was called out on a case and had to leave in a hurry." Joe, a forty-year veteran in the department with an exemplary record, had passed an intensive interrogation and lie detector test about that night. And though Scott had done so as well, the suspicion had still shifted back to him.

"It was just a bad deal, all around," Bob muttered. "Makes you wonder about who you can trust."

"And those surveillance tapes of someone making an ATM deposit into my account weren't of me." Scott heard the edge in his own voice and took a steadying breath. "Even in the poor lighting, it was clear the guy was at least three inches shorter and fifty pounds heavier. Like I said, Internal Affairs closed the investigation. End of story."

"I know, buddy. I know." Bob heaved a sigh. "I just wanted to give you a heads-up, so you'd know that things back here aren't exactly over."

Great.

Long after the call ended, Scott paced the aisle of the barn, cleaning stalls, lost in thought, feeling an overpowering urge to drive back to Chicago and face those rumors head-on. He'd been cleared once before, and still someone felt the need to stir things up. *Why?*

His nerves on edge, he glanced at his watch, then whistled to Jasper.

It was a four-hour drive to Billings. Home Depot should be open late on a Saturday night, and he could easily make it there in time to pick up a generator for all the times when the howling wind and fierce Montana storms knocked out his electrical service. Going somewhere—anywhere—was better than staying out here, alone with his thoughts. He could get back by midnight, if everything went well.

The old dog bounded toward him from a distant point in the meadow beyond the barn. "Come on, Jasper, let's hit the road."

Megan reached up to shift her wig of brunette hair and ran a fingertip over her crimson lipstick, then took a deep breath and rapped on the door to Hal Porter's office. This was a good idea. She knew it was—but convincing the brass was a whole different thing.

When he barked, "Come in," she strolled into his office and planted a hand on her hip, waiting for him to look up from his laptop.

He glanced up, still tapping on the keys. His

hands stilled as his brows drew together, his smile of welcome fading. He quickly masked the flicker of distaste in his eyes. "You'll have to stop at the secretary's desk, ma'am."

Yes! She tipped her chin up and gave her hair a sultry toss, not taking her eyes from his until she saw recognition dawn in his expression.

He tipped back in his chair, his hands braced on the armrests. "I thought we already talked about this, Megan."

"You said you didn't want me to go out on my own."

He leveled a long, steely look at her. "I just don't like it. This isn't some big city department with a team of undercover agents. We're short three full-time officers right now, and we don't have the manpower for backup. And if our suspect is a local, he'll recognize you."

She compressed her lips, holding back a snort of disbelief. "I don't cover the part of the county where the last victim lived, so few of those residents would recognize me. And even you didn't recognize me at first, right?"

"It took a minute, because you were silhouetted in the doorway," he growled.

"So in some dark, smoky bar, what are the chances?"

"Even if the killer doesn't recognize you, someone else might—and could inadvertently blow your cover right there. Worse, your credibility would be shot."

"Better that than another innocent woman, in the most literal sense," she retorted. "Think about it, boss."

"I have. The answer is still no."

"There's *nothing* I want more than to take this guy down. Give me one night...just one. Tonight. Ewan Baker says he'll be my backup."

Hal sighed. "Ewan."

Ewan wasn't her first choice, either, but she could handle herself and didn't expect trouble at any rate. "That's his part of the county. I'll troll out at the Halfway House—the place Dee Kirby visited last. She went there a number of times before she was killed, and always on Saturday nights. Give me midnight to two, then I'll be out of there, I promise." She saw the flicker of hesitation in Hal's eyes and took a deep breath before driving her point home. "Even if someone makes my identity, it's still all for the good. Word will spread that we're upping our efforts. It might make the killer think twice before trying anything more in Marshall County."

"Well…"

"I figure this guy scouts his victims in advance. Targets his quarry—maybe even follows them home. He wants to make sure he's ready when the next full moon rises. And I figure that gives us until June fifth. Twenty days."

"Maybe that timing has been a coincidence. If he's local, maybe he's already aware of the investigation, got cold feet and moved on."

"Or not. But I'm not willing to sit back and take that risk. Are you?"

Hal's face, folded into heavy wrinkles on the best of days, seemed to age before her eyes. "You won't take any chances?"

Curbing her rising impatience, she shook her head. He had always been a good boss. Honest, fair. Hardworking to a fault. But she'd been the first female deputy in the county, and he'd adopted a thinly veiled protective, grandfatherly air toward her from the first day she'd come on the job—one that had brought no end of subtle ribbing from her fellow deputies.

Still, though the line had never been crossed between appropriate, professional distance and true friendship, a small part of her heart—one that never experienced a father's attention—still took pleasure in his older-generation courtliness.

Before he could change his mind, she headed out the door. "Thanks."

He wasn't going to be sorry.

She was a lot better at her job than he gave her credit for, but this wasn't about proving her worth.

It was about the ghosts of her childhood that still haunted her thoughts. Ghosts that she still needed to put to rest. Maybe the vicious killer who'd murdered her cousin Laura fifteen years ago was long dead, but her overwhelming feelings of anger and helplessness remained—still roiling at the edges of her thoughts during every murder investigation.

Only now, it was far more personal.

An animal was preying on women. Picking them off, one by one. But this time, she was an experienced deputy, not a child. A crack shot. A woman ready to focus her fury and need for justice on the man who dared spread that same kind of terror through the county.

And if it was the last thing she ever did, she was going to take him down.

FIVE

After checking in with Ewan by cell phone, Megan tipped down the visor to study the stranger facing her in the dimly lit mirror, then applied another coat of lipstick and fluffed the thick bangs of her dark wig.

Even in the chilly night air, the wig was hot, and her false eyelashes—applied after studying a YouTube instructional video—felt like twin spiders perched on her eyelids.

With all the big hair, makeup, flashy red sweater and crimson fingertips, she was probably more ready for a costume party than a night on the town, even if Ewan *had* whistled in appreciation.

She tottered a few steps after leaving the truck, unaccustomed to high heels of any sort, then forced herself to walk slowly, smoothly to the door of the Halfway House Tavern. Loud music and raucous voices burst into the still night air as two cowboys staggered outside, one guy's arm looped around his buddy's shoulders. Both looked too drunk to walk.

She drew back in the shadows, watching to see if either of them got behind the wheel of one of the dozens of pickups nosed up to the outside of the building, ready to alert Ewan if either started to drive away. But they stumbled out into the darkness and sat on the open tailgate of one of the pickups, lighting up cigarettes and passing a crumpled brown paper bag between them.

Another battered pickup roared into the parking lot, kicking up a rooster tail of gravel that pinged against the vehicles closest to the highway as the driver turned hard, spun out, then lurched into an empty spot.

Two lanky young cowboys—barely legal and half-drunk, unless she missed her guess—loped to the entrance of the ramshackle tavern and disappeared inside.

Now, through the swinging door, she could see the shoulder-to-shoulder crowd milling about near the bar and caught glimpses of couples doing the Texas two-step or swing. Music blared from a makeshift bandstand in the back, where a trio of balding guys was manhandling a couple of guitars and a drum set with a lot of energy, but not a lot of talent.

Please, God…help me get through this all right. It's the last place I want to be.

Sure, she'd been in plenty of dives like this one with her badge and uniform on, breaking up fights, arresting drunks or collaring some guy with a warrant in hand, but if she wasn't careful, her discomfort as a "civilian" would be obvious to every last cowpoke in the place, even if they *were* drunk.

She hesitated at the door and took a deep breath. And realized that potential underage drinkers weren't the only reason to send Ewan back here. Along with the smell of old grease, probably from a limited bar menu, a haze of cigarette smoke—illegal in public places, per Montana law—drifted out into the night.

Smothering a cough, she stepped into the entryway.

A sun-browned cowboy loomed close, a wide grin revealing tobacco-stained teeth. "Hey, purty lady—where'd *you* come from?"

Another raised a glass in her direction, his eyes glazed. "Buy ya a drink, ma'am?"

Both of them were wiry and weathered to the hue of old leather. Maybe they were stronger than they looked, but neither had the calculating look in his eye that she'd hoped to find, or had the kind of build that could easily drag a body up a half mile of rugged trail.

She leaned close and lowered her voice. "Thanks. But I'm looking for a friend. A real big guy named—" she thought fast "—Bull Carraway. Real jealous guy, if you know what I mean."

The two aging cowhands melted back into the crowd.

She pressed on, slipping through a trio of grizzled men in well-worn shirts and dusty boots. Past a couple of fresh-faced young cowboys, their faces sunburned, foreheads white as fresh cream, who blushed deeper red and ducked their heads, tongue-tied and shy, as she passed.

A sense that she was being watched crawled up her back.

She eased farther into the crowd, angled toward a corner and glanced back, but saw no one staring at her—just a milling crowd that had closed in behind her, voices raised to be heard over the driving beat of some honky-tonk song she didn't recognize.

Someone bumped into her and she wobbled on her high heels, tipping precariously before she could grab for a post near the end of the bar.

"Having fun?" A low voice growled against her ear, the man's big hand settling possessively at the small of her back to steady her. "Fancy lady like you doesn't belong in a place like this."

She froze. Then forced herself to relax and smile, remembering her ruse. "I just thought I'd like to get out for a while. I like the band, don't you?"

She turned partway and found herself looking into the hard eyes of a man dressed better than most of the others. Western-cut blazer. Pressed slacks. Custom boots. A slick, confident smile on his full lips, though his belly bulged over his belt and strained the buttons of his shirt, and his heavy jowls swelled over his collar. His smile stretched faint scar lines over his nose and left cheek.

She pursed her mouth into a pout. "My fiancé is such a drag, sometimes. He'd rather stay home and watch the sports channel than have some fun."

The man bared his teeth in a wolfish smile. "Sounds boring to me."

She frowned and rested a hand on her hip. "Are you from around here? I don't think I've seen you before."

He pulled a business card from his pocket, his smile morphing into one of self-satisfaction, as if he was already sure she was his for the night. "Milt Powers. Insurance executive, actually. I come through this area several times a year. Want a drink?"

She quelled the urge to roll her eyes. *Executive—my foot.* He'd looked like a possibility at first, but his travels didn't parallel what she was looking for, and the gold-embossed card was one for a company that did advertise in Montana. The logo matched the TV ads and even bore his smiling face, name and address. Hardly what he'd share if he were trying for anonymity.

She offered an apologetic smile. "I don't think so. My…um…fiancé said he'd stop by later. Promised me one dance before I have to go home."

The interest in his eyes evaporated. With a shrug, he turned back to a blowsy redhead at the bar, and Megan moved on, slowly winding her way through the deepening haze of smoke, hiding her careful survey of the patrons with what she hoped was an air of a woman on the prowl.

Again, she felt someone staring at her, the sensation boring through her spine, and she turned slowly. Caught the eye of a few cowboys who grinned drunkenly back and raised their beer bottles at her. But…it wasn't them.

A beefy rancher-type, mid-forties with a bottle in his hand, gave her a once-over and edged through the crowd in her direction, the set of his jaw giving him the air of a pit bull establishing his territory. A path opened up for him, no one quite meeting his eyes.

Was it his gaze she'd felt? He was the best prospect so far, though she still couldn't shake her awareness of someone else—someone watching her with an intensity that made her shiver.

"Hey there," she purred. "Nice shirt."

He didn't spare a glance downward at what he wore. "You meeting someone?"

"Well..."

"You came in alone. Want a drink?"

"I came for the music, really. Maybe later."

He grabbed her arm and steered her toward an empty booth in an even darker corner of the tavern, jerking his jaw at the man behind the bar and lifting his nearly empty beer bottle as they passed. "So what's a girl like you doing here alone?"

She'd already heard the same line from Mr. Insurance, but from this man it was laden with far more intent. "I just wanted to get out. I don't come to places like this much at all, and it's kind of fun. Not something my fiancé likes, though so I have to go alone."

The barkeeper arrived with a new bottle of Coors and scurried away.

"Not much of a fiancé if he doesn't mind. Then again, what he doesn't know won't hurt him, eh?" He'd released her arm when they settled opposite each other in the booth. But now, he snagged her left hand again, turned it over and ran his thumb up and down her ring finger. "Too cheap for a diamond, I take it."

Realizing her mistake, she tried to pull her hand away, but he held fast, his grip tightening.

"I…we both wanted matching gold bands. Nothing fancy." She laughed lightly. "That costs too much, anyway, until he finds a better job. By the way—what's your name?"

"Lane."

"First or last?" She teased.

He ignored her question. "So…what are you doing the rest of the night? Want to check out The Drover on the other side of Copper Cliff? Better live band, and they serve good steaks."

He was big. A good two-forty, maybe five foot-eleven, with a potential for being aggressive, if his grip was any clue. She'd taken down bigger men than him in the past, but the thought of a wrestling match outside wasn't pleasant…and it would sure blow her cover for the future if she had to cuff him in front of any cowboys out there.

"Can't. Sorry." She gave him an apologetic

smile. “I’ve got someone stopping in a little later.”

His gaze hardened. “Who?”

She’d mentioned a burly boyfriend when she’d first walked in, then she’d referred to her fiancé. The latter seemed like the better choice now. This guy would probably want to stick around and challenge another rough, tough dude, and maybe go toe to toe. “My fiancé…once his…um…baseball game is over. Maybe.”

“I haven’t met him, but I know you could do better. Way better.”

She tilted her head. “Do you come here often?”

“Now and then.”

There was something about the man that made goose bumps rise on her arms, and it wasn’t because he was attractive. “Then maybe I’ll see you around here again, sometime.”

She started to rise, but he tightened his grip, twisting his wrist so she half fell back into the booth. “You don’t need to leave. I think we should talk awhile.”

“There are a lot of people here, mister. Maybe you’d better let go.”

The place was packed, but no one was looking in their direction. Beyond the booth, a faint incandescent bulb flickered over an exit sign at the end of a short, dark hallway.

Was this man her quarry?

Could he have hustled an intimidated woman out the rear door without being noticed? Had he flirted with Dee Kirby long enough to entice her into slipping out the back door with him?

Lane's mouth curved into a seductive smile. "I want to get to know you better."

The shadow of a tall, broad-shouldered man, silhouetted by the distant, faint glow of the neon beer signs over the bar, fell across the table, startling her.

"Let's go, sugar," the stranger said at her shoulder, in a deep voice that was oddly familiar. "You've had enough fun for tonight."

"She ain't going anywhere. She's with me."

"Actually, she isn't." The stranger's voice went even lower, his tone laced with lethal promise. "And if you don't want trouble, you'll let go of the lady's wrist and just sit back, nice and easy, while we leave."

Lane glared up at him. "You have no idea who you're talking to."

"And neither do you. You want to lose your pride in front of all these good folks, that's okay by me. Your choice."

After a long hesitation, Lane made a sound of disgust and dropped her wrist. "She's not worth the bother, cowboy. For you *or* me."

"Go ahead and believe it. It's in your best interest." The stranger touched her shoulder. "Let's go."

She didn't want to go, not yet. But now she'd placed the voice, and knew he might blow her cover if she balked. Some of the other cowboys had turned to look their way, so she played it cool. "Sure. Whatever."

He gently caught her hand and led her through the crowd, stopping only when they got to the front door. She glanced at the cowboys who were a little too close for comfort, then pulled her hand free and stepped outside.

He followed her to the shadowed side of the building and leaned a shoulder against the wall, as if he was just any cowboy flirting on a

Saturday night. "Well, then." His mouth tipped into a lazy smile. "Howdy, ma'am."

She scanned the area for anyone within earshot of their conversation, but there was no one in sight. "Don't 'howdy' me, Anders. You shouldn't have done that."

"You looked like you were in a little trouble back there, and I figured you could use some help." His gaze drifted up to her hair, and his mouth twitched. "Nice hairdo."

"You know what I do. You could've guessed I was working," she hissed. "What are you doing here?"

Her words echoed back to her, setting off alarm bells in her head. What *was* he doing here this late at night—here, of all places? Her stomach tightened at the possibilities—most of which weren't good.

"Rescuing a damsel in distress?"

"You ought to know it wasn't necessary."

"Right. That guy was inviting you to a tea party." His voice hardened. "So where is your backup?"

"As close as my cell phone."

"Not good enough. No matter how tough you think you are, that guy was twice your size and twice as strong. Factor in the testosterone and adrenaline rush fueling him, and—"

"A male deputy would've been in just as much trouble, if there was a fight. Don't start with the gender bias stuff. Please."

Scott held up his hands in mock surrender. "Sorry. My mistake."

"Do you come here often?"

"First time."

"*Really*. Sort of far, isn't it? You've got to live over an hour away, maybe more, given these mountain roads."

He shrugged. "Passing through."

Late on Saturday night? "From where to where?"

"What—is it illegal to be here?" He shook his head in disgust. "Come out and check my truck. I've got a receipt for the portable generator I picked up this evening in Billings. My dog is in the front seat, waiting for this."

He held up his other hand, and she realized that until now he'd held his hand at his side, and she hadn't noticed the small brown paper bag he was carrying. "W-what's that?"

"Two cheeseburgers and fries—half for

Jasper, half for me. That's the extent of the bar menu here. It was advertised as 'Good Eats' on a highway sign a mile north, and that sounded like gourmet fare to me, since I didn't stop for supper back in Billings."

A pure, warm sense of relief washed through her. "You stopped here for supper."

"Is that a problem?"

"O-of course not." She reached up to adjust her hair and caught another flicker of amusement in his eyes. "What?"

"Great outfit."

"But you knew me, even in that bad lighting," she said in disgust. "I wonder if anyone else did."

"I doubt it, but it would take more than a wig and caterpillars on your eyelids for me to miss someone like you," he said with a faint, enigmatic smile. "I'd recognize your profile and your attitude anywhere."

"Thanks."

"I kept an eye on things once I saw you because you seemed to be stirring up an awful lot of masculine interest over the 'floozy' in their midst. But don't worry—if anyone had recognized you as a deputy, the word would've spread fast."

"Because of the smoking violations and some underage drinkers in there, I suppose. And I can only imagine what else." She sighed. "Not exactly what I was after, but I'll make sure Ewan follows up. It's his territory."

She suddenly knew that Scott had been the man she'd sensed watching her back there, not the unknown killer she'd hoped was marking his next prey. If the insurance guy and the surly rancher didn't pan out, then the night had been a failure. Well, it had been a long shot, anyway.

"Since the boys inside must assume that I'm the mysterious fiancé I heard about, I don't suppose it'll look strange if I walk you to your truck." He cracked a smile and tipped his head toward the unlit perimeter of the lot, where she'd parked. "Do you mind?"

"I don't need protection." She started for her truck and he fell in step with her.

"Never thought you did. I just figured it would be better to get you out of there before you blew your cover, and had that jerk belly down on the floor with his hands cuffed behind his back."

"Now there's a pleasing thought." She knew he was just honoring her pride, though he'd truly thought she needed help. If it had been Hal, Ewan or any of the other guys, she would have been offended. But from Scott the interference felt different, and now a small, warm ember started to burn deep in her heart.

And with it, a measure of guilt.

"I'm sorry."

"About what?"

"For jumping to conclusions, back there." She bit her lower lip. "For questioning you about why you were here."

He shrugged. "It's your job to cover all the bases. Sometimes the most serious offenders can appear to be as innocent as lambs."

"But I should know better. You have no priors of any kind. And I know what you do—or did, in your career before coming here."

"When you make a career of investigating people, it's hard to put the doubts and suspicion aside." Something akin to pain flickered in his eyes, gone almost too quickly for her to catch. “Sometimes it’s safer not to.”

A couple of cowboys ambled out of the tavern and headed for opposite ends of the parking lot. These two, at least, looked as if they were steady on their feet.

Scott glanced down at what she held at her side. “Souvenir?”

“Sort of.” She lifted a shoulder. “Since it’s been *such* a lovely night, and all.”

With luck, she’d be able to lift Lane’s prints off his beer bottle and find some sort of record on him in the national AFIS registry. The knowing look in Scott’s eyes told her he knew exactly what she planned to do.

He walked with her, casually making conversation until she was in her pickup, the doors locked and the driver’s side window rolled down. “Take care, you hear? Stay out of trouble.”

“My job is taking *care* of trouble, Anders. Not avoiding it.”

“No insult intended. Just…take care.”

“I appreciate your concern, and I don’t mean to sound ungrateful. But please understand that I don’t need help, and I don’t need someone to watch over me. I've done my job for years now, as well as any man in the department—and better than some."

He lingered briefly, as if he wanted to say more, and in that silent, breathless moment she had a sudden image of him leaning closer. Meeting him partway…

But then his mouth broke into another faint smile. "As you wish, ma'am. Sorry I got in the way. I'll make sure I don't make the same mistake again." He sauntered away and disappeared into the night.

She rolled up her window and stared after him, then focused on the tavern, where lights pulsed at the windows and the muffled music seemed to shake the roof. This bar wasn't the only possibility. There were other places like this, that some of the victims had frequented before their deaths. Even so, their propensity for seeking out the wild side on Saturday nights might not have had any connection at all to the killer.

He could be a convenience store clerk.

A ski bum, hanging around the area for the winter.

A teacher or cowhand or anyone else.

He could be someone she knew well…and there were just twenty days left until the next full moon.

She had an entire county to cover. A county filled with some of the most rugged terrain in this hemisphere, where there were endless places to hide. *God, help me find this guy. And please, help me do it before another innocent woman dies.*

SIX

Megan pulled into her long, curving driveway at two in the morning, feeling as if she'd downed an overload of caffeine. Her thoughts raced back through the evening, over and over.

Had she missed anything at the Halfway House Tavern?

Skimmed past the killer's face without any sense of the evil that lurked behind a casual smile or offhand glance?

All the way home, she'd checked her rearview mirror hoping to see the twin pinpricks of light signifying that someone was following her. A couple times, she'd thought she saw exactly that—but then the lights turned off onto some side road and disappeared.

She had to be the only woman on the planet

who was disappointed that she hadn't picked up a stalker.

Turning off the ignition, she speed-dialed Ewan and told him she'd come up dry, though he'd need to start monitoring that tavern far more closely for bar license violations and the potential for drunk drivers.

She stepped out of her truck and surveyed the chain-link fenced yard for any motion, anything out of place. Tall pine trees crowded close to the rustic, single-story cabin, filtering the moonlight and casting dark shadows despite the single security light over the garage out in back.

The air was still, hushed, as if holding its breath and waiting for something to happen. The silence and eerie isolation of the place pressed in on her as she let herself through the gate and walked to the front door. She unlocked it, then reached inside the door to flip on the porch and interior lights and stood in the open doorway to survey the great room.

Everything was as it had been when she left.

The bright red-and-blue patchwork quilts

were still draped over the backs of the sofa and loveseat arranged in front of the stone fireplace. The comfy pair of overstuffed chairs were still in place in the opposite corner, facing the television she rarely had time to watch. And her beloved, original paintings of the Tetons still hung on the walls, done by a local artist she adored.

She breathed a sigh of relief, laughing off her momentary doubts. And then she froze.

Behind her, she heard the distant low growl of a motor.

The fading crunch of tires on gravel.

She spun around and stared into the darkness, then raced outside back to her truck.

Even on the darkest cloudy nights, the glow of headlights passing on the highway were masked by the curves of the quarter-mile driveway snaking through the dense pine forest. Only the loudest of the timber company trucks hauling massive logs could be heard at her cabin.

Yet she'd heard this vehicle, plain as day.

Whoever was out there hadn't just been passing on the highway. He'd been closer. In her *driveway.* Yet hadn't come on up to the cabin, as an acquaintance would do.

It had sounded as though the vehicle was leaving…though the driver could be parking it out of sight, planning to come back on foot. Unless he'd discovered everything he needed to know by just following her and seeing her name and rural address on the mailbox.

Swiftly climbing behind the wheel, she drove toward the highway with her headlights off, using just the moonlight as her guide, slowing to check every possible turnoff along the way.

When she reached the highway, she edged forward slowly, watching for any movement.

Nothing.

Frustrated, she drummed her fingers on the steering wheel and stared at the empty road. If that vehicle belonged to her suspect and he thought she was easy prey, he'd have a big surprise. Anticipation and determination made her muscles tense, heightening her senses and awareness of the vast, empty forest surrounding her. Made her long for that confrontation; for the final resolution of the case.

Still, the thought of a watchful night ahead,

when an intruder could so easily slip up to her cabin, unseen in the darkness, set her nerves on edge.

She waited another ten minutes, then drove slowly back home. Pulling to a stop near the front door, she glanced at her patrol car parked nearby, still emblazoned with K-9 unit on the side. Now, she missed her dog more than ever. She'd been blessed with the county's only drug dog for over four years, until Charger was shot during a meth lab bust six months ago that had left Charger with a bullet in the chest.

He'd been her constant companion, her partner. Her best friend. Until now, the thought of replacing him had made her heart clench… though the county had no money to purchase a new dog, at any rate.

But any dog would offer the comfort of sharp ears and a loud bark. Why hadn't she moved past her sorrow and found one sooner?

At the door of the cabin, she stood in the entryway as the minutes ticked by, straining to hear any sound of someone approaching. Only the faint cry of an owl broke the silence.

Now, a fitful breeze picked up, rushing through the pines and rustling the leaves of the aspens into a host of delicate castanets behind the house.

Chilled, she finally let herself inside and shoved the dead bolt home. She walked through the main floor, closing curtains and locking windows in the two small bedrooms and great room, then she double-checked the back door and windows in the kitchen. Securely locked, as always.

"Nothing to worry about," she told herself, speaking aloud into the silence. "Nothing at all."

Maybe that car had simply belonged to someone who had taken a wrong turn, stopped in her drive to double-check a map or GPS, then backed out and left.

But how often did even a single car pass by on these isolated roads at night? And the timing, right after her undercover search at the tavern, was too coincidental to ignore.

She wouldn't bet her life on that car belonging to someone who was lost.

Heading for her main floor bedroom, she reached up in the closet and pulled her service revolver from its locked case. Loaded it. Then she gave her ankle holster a pat for reassurance before settling on the sofa with a pillow and blanket, the exterior lights all blazing at both the front and back doors.

It was time to visit her childhood friend Kris down in Battle Creek. Maybe even after church later this morning…

Before she had too much time to think about all the reasons why it would be a very bad idea.

"I can't believe it!" Kris Donaldson rushed forward and gave Megan a hug, then held her at arm's length and frowned, her lovely, honey-brown eyes filling with concern. "You look exhausted. What's up?"

"Late night." A sleepless one, listening for footsteps outside, but sharing that bit of news would lead to too many questions. "You look fantastic."

"I couldn't be happier." She waved a hand toward the newly finished cabin behind her, and the long kennel building and barns at the other end of the meadow. "I got to move into the new cabin just this past week. And best of all, I just heard from the County Board of Supervisors. They're pleased with how the animal shelter has been operating here, and said they're already planning to extend my contract for another three years."

"After everything you went through last winter, you deserve good news. Congratulations." Megan grinned. "Now, tell me about that cowboy of yours. Is he still around?"

Kris blushed. "Quite a bit. Trace and I are 'an item' according to his sister Carrie. She teases us about it all the time and swears that if he doesn't propose by the end of the year, she'll eat her best boots—and she'll also disown him."

"I'm so happy for you. He seems like a great guy."

"Do you have time for dinner? Carrie invited Trace and me over to her place at two, for her incredible coconut cake and fried chicken. Even if it isn't exactly heart-healthy, we're celebrating his birthday today and it's Trace's favorite meal."

Megan glanced at her watch. "Sounds fantastic, but I need to get back to Copper Cliff. I…wonder if I could see some of your dogs."

"Absolutely. Are you looking for anything

in particular?" Her eyes sparkled. "Something small and fluffy?"

"You know me so well," Megan said with a dry laugh. "How about something like that, times three?"

"We're actually really full right now, so you'll have a lot to choose from." Kris led her down to the kennels, opened the door and ushered her inside. "You might wish you had earplugs."

The inmates burst into a deafening chorus of barking, some of the dogs launching themselves at the wire mesh doors of their runs, while others cowered at the back.

"Let's start at one end and work our way down," Kris said, raising her voice to be heard above the din. "Some of them are quite new, so I don't know as much about them yet. They aren't available until I can assess their behavior and personality for being a safe pet."

"What are the adoption arrangements here?"

"A seven-day waiting period after your decision. A signed contract, promising the animal won't be given away or sold. The dogs are vaccinated and spayed or neutered before leaving."

Megan's heart fell. "Seven days?"

"I can make rare exceptions. For you, as an example. You live a long ways from here. And I know you'd give an animal a wonderful home."

Megan followed her to the end of the building, then walked slowly, surveying the runs on both sides of the aisle. "You sure have a lot of puppies."

"Are you looking for something young?"

"Grown. Something with a good bark and protective tendencies, but not a breed I'd have to worry about with visitors—especially children."

Kris tapped her lips with a forefinger. "I know you like bigger dogs. We've got a couple of labs—both are older animals, though. Several larger mixed breeds."

"Sounds good."

She paused in front of one of the cages and hunkered down to entice the golden retriever closer. "This one is a sad case. He was found with a collar practically embedded in his neck, and he was so undernourished that I figure he was dumped and on his own for a long time. He's still so, so thin. We try to feed him a lot, but he just isn't thriving in this environment."

"It's unbelievable, how selfish and cruel people can be."

"And he probably saw some of the worst. But unfortunately, even now he won't have a chance to finish his life in a loving home. He's at least eight, maybe nine, so adoptive families will be leery of looming geriatric issues."

Megan nodded. "That's so sad."

"It sounds like you need a young, vigorous dog, at any rate, so you wouldn't want to deal with his problems. Someone will have to work at gaining his trust, and that could take a long time. He was already neutered when he came in, but I don't even know if he's housebroken."

"Poor guy. Goldens are such sweet dogs." Megan moved on to the next pen, where a German shepherd whined and pawed at the door of his run. He was massive, clearly in his prime. "This one looks like a good possibility." When she started to pass by, he erupted into a frenzy of deafening barks. "A definite possibility."

But even with all of the German shepherd's ideal qualities, her gaze strayed back to the golden. He was staring at her with such a look of hopelessness and heartbreak in his eyes, that she felt her own heart melt into a puddle at her feet.

She studied him, taking in the abuse he'd suffered. The quiet dignity in the way he sat still, his eyes fixed on hers, while most of the others were going crazy for attention.

"I wonder if he'd even have the spirit left to be a good watchdog, or if he'd just be afraid and cower."

"He's terrified of men, but after surviving on his own, I think he'd be even more protective of his home than most. But he'd also be patient with children and any visitors he saw you welcome. Goldens are like that. My old Bailey has the fiercest bark you can imagine, and you know what a lamb he is otherwise."

Megan moved back to stand in front of his cage, flipped the latch and opened the door. She hunkered down. "Here, buddy."

He studied her as if searching her very soul,

before he finally rose and limped toward her, slowly closing the distance between them. After a long moment, he solemnly sat down and lifted a paw to rest it on her knee, never taking his eyes from hers.

It was like a promise.

A promise that if she'd only love him back, he'd love her forever, with all his heart. That he'd give his life for hers and never think twice.

And in that moment, she knew that no other dog would do.

She cradled his head in her hands. "You're it, buddy. You just found yourself a home."

Scott hefted a quarter-bale of hay, judged the distance, and launched it over the fence. It landed dead center in the hay bunk in Attila's corral.

The donkey waggled his good ear. Moved forward to sniff his dinner. Then he sidestepped around it to hang his head over the fence and stare longingly at the cabin.

After his first assault on the roses, he'd managed to escape almost every day, even after Scott had added a high set of planks on the fence.

One by one, the roses bloomed—and within twenty-four hours they each disappeared.

He was the most single-minded creature Scott had ever met.

"You and Officer Peters are a lot alike," Scott muttered as he double-checked the chain on the gate.

The way his blood had chilled at seeing her in that seedy tavern still made him shiver. He hadn't asked why she was there. It hadn't been hard to guess. She was searching for leads in that murder case.

But to go into that place without backup within shouting distance was flat-out reckless.

Before he'd been in there five minutes he'd seen cowboys too drunk to know what they were doing—too drunk to remember anything the next day.

And he'd seen prison tats on a couple of guys with cold, hard eyes and six-inch knives on their belts. Maybe they were just passing through. Maybe they were lying low, working in the back of beyond on some ranch. But a pretty woman alone could be bait enough for them to take chances. No matter what she thought, Megan would have been in a vulnerable position if she'd caught their eye.

And the man she'd sat with in that booth had looked like pure trouble.

She'd made it clear that she didn't want Scott's help, and he'd left the world of law enforcement behind for good. So why did he feel this persistent compulsion to check up on her, just to make sure she was safe?

"Not my business," he reminded himself aloud.

Attila looked at him and flapped his lips, making a whuffling noise that almost sounded like a chuckle.

"Thanks, pal."

The donkey lifted his head to look over Scott's shoulder toward the lane, his good ear swiveled in that direction. A moment later, a patrol car came into view.

Scott felt his pulse pick up a faster beat that he tried to ignore. "She really, *really* isn't my business."

The vehicle crept past Jasper, who lifted his head in casual greeting before flopping back down in the dust. Megan pulled to a stop by the barn and stepped out, her khaki uniform sharply pressed, her service belt looking too heavy, too bulky for her slender waist. Dark aviator sunglasses masked her eyes, and she wasn't smiling.

"You back to checking out your number one suspect?" he drawled. "I'm beginning to think I'm the only one who's convenient."

"Thanks. My boss would be really pleased at that assessment. Convenience over accuracy—and it saves gas mileage, too." She slipped off her glasses and studied the donkey. "Had him long?"

"Does he need an alibi?"

Her lovely mouth twitched. "That depends. Has he been in any trouble?"

"His named is Attila, if that's any clue. And I didn't name him that, so he probably has a rap sheet a mile long."

"Did you bring him from Chicago?"

"He was…a spur of the moment decision. I went to a sale in February, wanting to buy a tractor. He was going for twenty-five bucks, and I was afraid he might end up in a semi-trailer, headed for the glue factory." Scott gave a rueful laugh. "Now I've got a donkey, no tractor and a rapidly disappearing rose garden. But I'm sure you would never make an emotional decision like mine."

"Nope." She cast a guilty glance over her shoulder at something moving on the front seat of the cruiser. "Never."

He squinted against the bright morning sunshine. "Did they give you a police dog to match the K-9 logo on your car?"

"Uh...no."

Curious, he strolled over and peered inside. A gaunt, white-muzzled golden retriever stared back at him and tentatively waved his tail. "Stray?"

"He was." She blushed a little. "I think he's now my new best friend. I wanted one who could also listen for intruders."

Scott frowned and turned around. *"Intruders?* Did you get him because you had trouble last night?"

"Someone may have followed me. I thought it could be you, just making sure I got home, but the car took off in a hurry. I would've called to ask you, but Information doesn't have you listed."

"It wasn't me. Jasper and I had our supper in my truck before we hit the road, so I was probably ten minutes behind you. And I went straight home because you made it clear that you didn't want any interference."

"Maybe it was just someone who got lost and turned around in my driveway."

"I hope so. Do you live alone?"

She nodded. "Now I wish I'd gone after him. If I'd moved faster, maybe I could've pulled him over, or at least gotten close enough so I could run his license plates."

And then maybe you'd be dead.

She was independent. She was armed. She was a sworn deputy with years of experience. But he still couldn't set aside his uneasy feelings about her safety. "I'm glad you didn't."

She frowned at him, and he could feel a cool wall rising up between them. "Then I'm glad you're not a partner of mine. You'd probably have me sitting back at the sheriff's office, out of harm's way."

"That's a great idea."

A faint twinkle glinted in her eyes. "Then remind me to never suggest that you look for a job with the county sheriff's department."

"You're safe. I can promise it will never be on my agenda." Though the thought of being able to keep an eye on her—in a purely professional way—did have some appeal. A host of grisly images crowded into his mind from the myriad cases he'd been involved with over the years. Killers without remorse. Those who took pleasure in orchestrating a terrifying death for their victims. "Just don't take any chances. As isolated as you are out here, you have no idea how truly evil men could be."

She snorted. "Don't kid yourself."

"Well...just in case you need backup sometime—" He grinned at her. "Or you want to check up on my latest nefarious pursuits, here's my cell number." He pulled a pen and scrap of paper from the breast pocket of his denim jacket, and wrote down his phone number. "I don't use a landline here."

She took it and punched it into her Contacts directory, then pocketed the slip of paper. "Thanks."

"So we're making some progress, I take it?"

She looked up. "What?"

"This is the first time you've actually suspected me of something *good*."

She laughed, a soft, silvery sound, as she slipped her sunglasses back into place and opened her car door. "My mistake. Make sure you toe the line, mister—because I'll be keeping an eye on you."

SEVEN

Scott paced the floor, then growled in frustration and settled down in front of his computer monitor, staring at the blank screen that had been mocking him since five in the morning.

Last night he'd tried staying up late, forcing himself to sit at his desk with his hands poised over the keyboard until he'd finally dredged up enough words to fill a page.

This morning he'd gotten up early to get the article done…but the words from the night before had all looked like drivel, and he'd erased the lot…only to discover that looking at a page of nonsense meant there was something to fix, but a blank page was worse—especially with a deadline of five o'clock on Monday and an auction he needed to attend this afternoon.

Back home in Chicago he'd written a couple of salable articles each month despite his fourteen-hour days on the job, his cramped home office and the high drama Olivia had brought into his life.

Here, he had a perfect office looking out at the mountains, all the time in the world, and the words just wouldn't come, even though rainy Sunday mornings had always seemed liked an ideal time for writing. His gaze settled on the barn, where just the tip of Attila's good ear was visible over the corral fence.

Fencing would be a good project for this weekend—if he went to town and picked up the fencing materials.

Though if he went to town, he'd have a good chance of running into Megan, because she seemed to turn up everywhere he went. And thinking about her was already occupying entirely too much of his thoughts already.

He stood, grabbed his keys and jacket, and headed out the door, whistling. Maybe if he *did* run into her, he'd see that she was perfectly fine, in no obvious trouble, and he could go back to his routine. He'd be able to concentrate, and get his writing done.

And then his life would go back to being exactly as he'd planned.

Megan settled onto one of the counter stools at Hannah's Pastries 'n' More. "A day off. Now, this is something to savor."

Sue Ann bustled over with a fat stainless steel coffeepot, grabbed a thick china mug from below the counter and poured her a cup. "And it has to be raining. Tough luck."

Megan shrugged. "Still, I'm here, and I can linger. I might go down to the bookstore in Lost Falls and just lose myself in those books for a while. Perfect thing for a rainy Sunday."

"The place with the tea and classical music?"

"That's it. They have a whole room filled with mysteries, thrillers and romantic suspense. By the time I leave, I've always bought way too many." A feeling of bliss came over her, and she smiled. "Just the smell of books and tea and their Irish Cream coffee makes me happy."

Sue Ann leaned closer, her eyes wide.

"Speaking of mysteries, anything new about those poor women who were murdered?"

If there were, Sue Ann would be the last person to tell, unless something needed to become common knowledge in a hurry. "We're working on it, and so is the state DCI unit."

Sue Ann lowered her voice. "I saw those guys, when they came to town. Hmm-mmm. They stopped here for lunch, and they were mighty fine. Will they be back?"

Only if someone else dies. "Hard to say," Megan said with a vague wave of her hand. "I just hope we catch the guy so they don't need to."

"The paper called him the Full Moon Killer." Sue Ann drew back, a hand fluttering at her neck. "But what if he strikes at random next time? I wish I could just leave here, and go stay with my sister in Oregon."

Megan had heard a number of other people talk about leaving town, and what the situation would do to the upcoming tourist season wasn't hard to guess. "The sheriff's department is following every lead, believe me."

"But that's what everybody's talking about

these days—how there don't seem to *be* any. How he could be one of us, and we don't even know it. Or how he could be someone new around here, who looks normal as can be. Like that new fella—he comes in here, now and then."

"I think we all just need to be calm, and careful and not jump to any conclusions. We have absolutely no suspicions about Mr. Anders," Megan retorted, a little too sharply. She steadied her voice. "No evidence whatsoever. I hope you aren't mentioning him to your customers. False accusations could stir up a lot of legal trouble for you."

"N-no. Of course not." Sue Ann cast a quick, guilty glance toward several patrons seated at the front windows. None of them looked up. "And I'll make sure to let people know, if I hear such talk."

Megan closed her eyes briefly. Though the woman had a good heart and would never mean any harm, damage control with Sue Ann was like trying to dam a river with chewing gum. "It would be better if you just didn't say anything at all."

"I won't. *I swear.*" The little bell over the

entryway tinkled as the door opened. Sue Ann's eyes widened and she sucked in a sharp breath. *"Oh."*

Megan looked up, already knowing who she'd see reflected in the long mirror behind the old-fashioned soda fountain. She gave Sue Ann a pointed look, then turned to him and smiled. "Scott."

"Megan." He stamped his boots on the entry mat and then sauntered up to her, the deep waves of his coal-black hair wet and gleaming from the rain, his light blue eyes more startling than ever in contrast to his lean, wind-burned face. A corner of his mouth twitched. "Let me guess," he added in a low tone only she could hear. "This is another undercover outfit?"

"Very funny." She watched Sue Ann move to the other patrons, coffeepot in hand. "It would be effective, though. Ninety percent of the people around here wear denim jackets and jeans, so I'd blend right in."

"Had any more unexpected visitors out at your place?"

"None—assuming that my new guard buddy has good ears."

"Do you keep him outside?"

"Goodness, no. It's chilly out there this time of year."

"He's probably used to it, if he was a stray."

"But he's older. He deserves to be inside, and he can bark just as well with a roof over his head. If someone tested the doors or windows, he'd sure let me know."

"True." Scott studied the toes of his boots for a moment, then looked up with a hopeful smile. "Are you working today?"

"Nope. This is a rare day off."

The dimples bracketing his mouth deepened. "Are you free?"

"Well...I do have plans. Sort of."

"Important?"

"Well..." She thought longingly of the bookstore.

On the other hand, a rugged version of Pierce Brosnan was now grinning at her with a hopeful expression in his eyes, and that opened up a set of entirely different possibilities. "Why do you ask?"

"I had to come into town to pick up some fencing materials, and now I'm heading to an estate sale south of Lost Falls." His low, self-deprecating laugh danced across her skin. “When I noticed your truck parked on the street, I figured it wouldn’t hurt to ask. Maybe you can keep me from doing something stupid.”

She glanced out the window at her pickup. Through the rain-streaked windshield, she could make out the vague, furry shape of her new best friend, who was sitting behind the wheel and who hadn’t taken his eyes off her since she sat down at the counter.

“We…may not actually agree on what constitutes a mistake,” she murmured.

Buddy was seeing the vet tomorrow because she was beginning to suspect hip dysplasia in the way he limped, poor guy. He could end up being a very *expensive* new best friend. But he definitely hadn’t been a *mistake*.

“Well, last time, I ended up with Attila the Donkey. There was just something about that floppy, broken ear…”

“If I say ‘no,’ you’d actually listen?”

He glanced down at the edge of her boot cut jeans draped loosely at the top of her running shoes. “You’re carrying, right? You could always threaten to arrest me.”

She thought about her bare bones cabin. She'd moved in six months ago, and had furnished it with just the basic necessities—except for the two paintings that had wiped out her budget for any other nonessentials for the foreseeable future.

"Are they selling household items, too?"

"Everything."

"Hmm." She'd been suspicious of him at first, and back then she might have welcomed an extended opportunity for subtle, leading questions. Now, the thought of simply getting to know him a little better—as a friend—just sounded like fun.

Most guys she met were intimidated by her, though they never admitted it aloud; their masculinity apparently threatened by a woman who packed a gun and could deal with bad guys twice as big and tough as they were. During her two longest relationships, that intimidation and her twelve-hour shifts through the night had eventually made Brad and Jon grow resentful.

But here was a man from her own world, for whom that wouldn't be a problem, and he was clearly looking for companionship and nothing more. Maybe a day like this *would* be fun—as two equals. Just casual camaraderie, without any illusions about any sort of romantic interest going on.

She slid off her stool and grabbed her purse. "Then I guess you have a deal…as long as my dog can come along."

The rain slowed to a light drizzle by the time they reached Lost Falls, then started up again with a vengeance as they wound through the foothills on a narrow, two-lane county road to the auction site.

A bedraggled group of bidders was crowded around an auctioneer and his assistants, who stood on a hay wagon stacked with smaller items, while farther up the steep hill, an old tractor, wagons and various implements were lined up for viewing.

Beyond that, a split rail corral held a small assortment of livestock that stood in the lee of a crumbling old barn weathered to pale silver.

Scott waited while Megan let Buddy out of the truck to do his business, then helped him up into the backseat again, where he'd be out of the rain. "It's unbelievable that someone could have abandoned a dog like him."

"If I knew who they were, I'd try to arrest them for animal cruelty. The sad thing is that the charges don't carry strong enough penalties, and the owners could convince a judge that the dog simply ran off." Shivering, she zipped the front of her rain jacket and pulled up the hood. "The thing is, I don't think a sweet old dog like this would've gone miles and miles into uninhabited forest, away from all the campgrounds and resorts. I still think he was ditched."

Scott nodded. "Maybe the vet can check to see if he was microchipped."

"Good idea." She fell in step with him on the overgrown lane leading up to the barn and house. "So, what are you after here, besides a tractor?"

"Implements. Hand tools. Shovels, rakes… pretty much anything I can find. And you?"

She made a face. "It's probably time that I found more kitchen stuff and started doing a little more cooking at home. With the hours I keep, I haven't bothered much."

They both stopped at a card table on the

front porch of the house to fill out forms and receive bidding numbers.

Scott put his in his shirt pocket, then buttoned up his long drover's coat. "I'm heading up the hill to check out the equipment. Want to come along?"

"In a bit. I'm going to grab a cup of hot chocolate at the food stand inside, then check out the household things."

"Sounds good." Bemused, she watched him step out in the rain and stride through the mud.

The miles had flown past on the way here. He'd been easy to talk to, though the silences had been just as comfortable as the conversation—as if they'd known each other for years.

Yet now she realized that he'd deftly kept the conversation in her court, and she didn't know much more about him now than she had before. By accident or design?

She turned to go inside and bumped into a woman with long blond hair who was easing out the door with a cup of steaming coffee in her hand. "Erin?"

The blonde looked up and her mouth

dropped open. "Megan—oh, my word!" She looked down at her coffee, laughing. "I want to give you a big hug. But I can't! How is everything?"

Megan stepped back outside, holding the door for her cousin. "Busy. And you?"

Erin gestured toward the hill with her coffee cup as they moved to the corner of the porch to allow others to pass by. "I came looking for garden tools. I'd like to grow fresh produce and herbs for the café next year. Jack—" She glanced over her shoulder "—is somewhere out there with his nephew. There's a sign on the barn offering free kittens."

Something on her left hand sparkled, catching the light from the bare lightbulb. Megan blinked then stared. "Erin!"

Blushing, Erin extended her hand. "It's new, just this weekend. Isn't it lovely? I meant to call you and Kris this week."

"Wow." Mindful of the hot coffee in Erin's hand, Megan gave her a hug, then stepped back. "It's amazing, isn't it? How life has changed?"

"I never thought I'd come back to Montana. Once I graduated from high school, I couldn't wait to get away. The memories were still so hard. And yet here I am again, running Grandma Millie's little general store. And I'm so happy now—it's like I had to come back home to finally heal."

Megan nodded. "I stopped in to see Kris yesterday. She's doing really well, too, since she moved back."

"We were quite something as kids, weren't we? She was always like a third cousin." Erin shook her head fondly. "I have a lot of great memories of those times…at least until the summer Laura died."

"Same here." Megan bit her lower lip. "Losing her like that changed us all."

Erin fell silent for a long moment. "You were the only one of us who didn't leave Montana."

"Hey," Megan protested. "I did move to the next county."

Erin's delicate eyebrows drew together. "Do you ever regret not getting away from here?"

"I'm doing exactly what I was meant to do. No regrets." A shadow crossed her thoughts… one born of an evil stranger's cunning that made her heartbeat stumble. "It's not all fun, believe me. But I'm doing the right thing. I'd rather try to make a difference than run."

Erin glanced over her shoulder, then lowered her voice. "I've been reading the news about those murders in the newspaper. Our tourist business is starting to trickle in, and even the vacationers have heard about them. Some stop by the store for supplies, but say they've decided to head south to the Tetons instead."

"I can promise you that we're doing everything we can, and the DCI has been involved, too. We're following up on every lead we get."

"Believe me, I'm not questioning what's being done. I'm just glad you're on board, and that the county has a sheriff who will do a good job. Do you remember the alcoholic we had back when we were kids?"

"Sheriff Nelson."

"I'll never forget how he bungled the investigation of Laura's murder. If he'd acted faster, maybe she would've been found in time—before that monster killed her. I only hope she didn't suffer too much."

Megan had seen the original reports, and Laura hadn't ever had a chance. But those terrible details were something she would never repeat to her cousin.

"The sheriff didn't even start *looking* for her for three days, insisting she was just a runaway. Yet just the month before, he'd been given information about a known pedophile who'd moved into the area and he didn't follow up. Apparently—" Megan tried to quell the bitterness rising in her voice. "He misplaced the report. He was probably busy hitting the booze or focusing on one of his wild kids. They were always getting kicked out of school."

"I remember. Kenny, Bobby and..." Erin frowned. "Randy...Rick..."

"Rex. Apparently Nelson wasn't too effective as a dad, either, because those kids were in constant trouble."

"Rex nearly died in that big meth lab explosion up at Copper Creek, didn't he?"

"Yep. But I've researched everything that happened around the time of Laura's death, and there's absolutely nothing about it in the files. Nelson apparently destroyed the records and the evidence to protect his son. It would've been easier back then because the records weren't computerized."

"It was a good day for the county when Nelson lost the next election for sheriff and they all moved away." Erin smiled sadly. "And maybe it gave the family a good fresh start somewhere else. I hope so."

"I hope so, too. I never heard another word about them after that, so they must have been fine. But Nelson was still my biggest motivation for going into law enforcement. I wanted to make sure that kind of incompetence never happened again. Not on my watch, at least."

A brief memory flashed through Megan's thoughts, of a warm, sunny day when she'd been in town all those years ago. The Nelsons had been driving out of town in a minivan, their faces grim. Rex, his face still ruddy with healing burns, had looked out the window. Though he was an older boy and she'd barely known him, she waved goodbye. He'd just scowled in return and mouthed some words she couldn't hear.

Probably just as well.

"My biggest fear is that you'll take too many chances and get hurt somehow. There are just too many crazy people out there." She rested a hand on Megan's forearm and squeezed tight. "Promise me you'll be careful."

Megan grimaced. "I keep hearing that from people these days."

From somewhere outside, a young boy started calling Erin's name in a high, excited voice.

"I think you're being paged."

Erin rolled her eyes, though the affection in her gaze was obvious. "Three guesses on what Max found."

Now Megan could see a young boy zigzagging through the crowd at a run, with Erin's fiancé in hot pursuit. "Erin! I found my kitty. Come quick! Erin!"

"You'd better go, future stepmom. I'll catch up with you later."

The sparkle in Erin's eyes matched the one on her left hand. "Don't forget—it'll be a small ceremony out at the lake, end of July. And I definitely want you in the wedding, if you're free."

"Absolutely." Megan watched her cousin step out into the rain to catch up with the eager child and Jack.

Erin bent down to give Max a hug, and then they all walked hand in hand toward the barn on the hill, Jack's arm draped around Erin's shoulders.

A family in the making.

Exactly what Erin had wanted, and Kris, too, back when they were all kids, playing house in the little cottage behind Grandma Millie's General Store out at the lake. It even looked like Kris was on the way to her own happy ending, too, which made Megan's heart expand with quiet joy for both of them.

Please, Lord, watch over them...bring them the happiness that escaped them for so long—be with them, and bless them. And please, keep them safe. Her bright spirits faded as quickly as they'd come.

The "keeping them safe" part was her department. But so far, she hadn't worked hard enough, hadn't been smart enough, hadn't been able to see the pattern and the clues clearly enough to stop that killer in his tracks.

Seventeen days until the next full moon.

And if she hadn't done her job well enough by then, someone else might die.

EIGHT

"I really didn't mean to buy a goat," Scott muttered, standing with one foot hitched on the bottom rail of the corral by the barn. "It just...happened."

In the background, the crowd had followed the auctioneer to a rusty, ancient vehicle, where he began his rapid-fire patter extolling all of its amazing qualities.

"Did you say you bought a *goat?*" He looked so grim that Megan tried to smother her laugh. "By accident?"

"A big one."

She followed his gaze to a white goat with impressive horns and a long beard. It appeared to be eating the fence. "Look—he's trying to spring all his buddies."

"I know. I'm sure he and Attila will get along just great."

"Not that it's my business, but how did this happen?"

"Some teenagers standing next to me were really upset. They were talking about how they'd miss their grandpa's hobby farm and all the animals he kept for them. One of the girls started crying, saying she'd caught some kids mercilessly teasing the goat and the other animals. When she tried to intervene, the kids said their parents were planning on buying every one of those animals, so she should mind her own business."

"So you bought the goat."

He cleared his throat. "And a pony."

"I really needed to get up here sooner, didn't I," she said solemnly. "Was there anything else?"

"The tractor…and a goose. Not much."

"A goose. How sweet. I think we need to get you home."

A corner of his mouth tilted up in a boyish grin. "The tractor is old, but it's perfect for what I need, and the price was right. This was a great sale."

She finally gave up and laughed. He'd seemed distant and even a little cold when she'd first met him, and until recently she'd even considered him a suspect in the Full Moon murders. Finding that his tough shell hid a soft heart made her like him all the more. "Maybe God was rewarding you for saving some of his creatures."

"I'm not sure He cares much about what I do. But if that's the case, I guess I'll accept it and be thankful."

Startled, she looked up at him.

He caught her expression. "Oh, I've been a believer since I was a child. My parents never miss a Sunday at church, and that's how I was raised. I'm just not so sure that God is listening to me anymore."

"But..."

"I worked the streets of Chicago, Megan. Tell me that violence and greed and injustice doesn't change you, if you see it every day. And if you've been in situations where a little intercession could've saved a life and God doesn't answer—then you start to figure that maybe you're in this alone."

Megan took a deep breath and led her old dog to the door of the vet clinic. She could feel his body trembling against her leg. "Whatever we have to face, we're a team now," she whispered. "And no matter what anyone says, I made the right decision when I brought you home."

He balked, then gave up and followed her inside, tagging along at the end of his leash, his head low and tail tucked between his legs. "It's okay, Buddy. Neva Baker is the nicest vet around. You'll see."

The old retriever's eyebrows wobbled up and down as he looked up at her, then he sighed heavily, his head resting on her thigh when she took a chair in the waiting room. He clearly trusted her, but he'd been trembling from head to tail since they first arrived in the clinic parking lot.

Now, if only the news here would be good.

"We're all set for you." Cara, the tall, slender vet tech, motioned them to come in. "Dr. Baker wants to do an exam, and then we might need some X-rays."

Megan led the dog into an exam room and helped the tech lift him onto a stainless steel table. A moment later, Neva bustled in wearing pale green scrubs. At almost forty, she was trim and petite, a pixie of a woman with the firm handshake of a lumberjack and the most infectious laugh Megan had ever heard.

She fixed Megan with a keen look. "I figured it wouldn't be long till we saw you again with another dog. What do we have here?"

"A friend runs the new shelter in Battle Creek. I was looking for a younger dog, but she figured this old guy was abandoned. He… well, he just looked like he needed a home."

"Do you have any health documents from the shelter?"

Megan pulled a set of folded papers from her purse. "He had a veterinary exam two weeks ago. He was previously neutered. They gave him tests for intestinal parasites and heartworm, plus his vaccinations for rabies, DHPP, Lyme and Bordetella."

Neva nodded her approval. "What about flea and tick prevention?"

"Done. Heartworm, too. He was anemic and seriously underweight, but he's been eating like a horse since I brought him home."

Neva cradled the dog's head in her hands and looked into his eyes. "That's what you needed, isn't it? Your own home. Does he have a name?"

"I guess I've mostly been calling him Buddy, for lack of anything else. Not very unique."

"It's a good name. We'll put that down for now." The vet looked up at Megan. "So tell me about his symptoms."

"I've only had him for a few days, but he seems stiff in the mornings and he limps during the day—especially after he first stands up. I just don't want him to be in pain."

Neva began her examination. "Does he do better after he's warmed up a little?"

"Some."

"When he runs, does he have an odd sort of bunny hop gait?"

"No. Not really."

She continued her exam by gently flexing Buddy's back legs. "This doesn't appear to hurt him, and his joints feel good and tight. I'd like to take a couple of radiographs, just to be sure, if that's okay?"

Megan nodded and stepped out of the room. She paced the waiting area for a half hour until Neva came out with Buddy at her side. "Is he all right?"

"Without sending the X-rays to a specialist, I can still safely say that he has some arthritis, but not dysplasia—which is good news. The sad news is that he shows evidence of an old hairline fracture of his femur, and has four healing rib fractures that are newer. He might have been kicked, or beaten or maybe hit by a car. It's too far out to tell, since the soft tissue damage has healed. He probably had deep bruising and was in a world of hurt while he was on his own."

Megan knelt at his side and gave his neck a gentle hug. "You poor baby."

"For more comfort with the arthritis, I'd make sure he has a soft, well-padded bed and has a warm place to sleep at night. Excess weight obviously isn't an issue now, but I wouldn't let him get heavy. Regular, mild exercise every day. I've got a good glucosamine-chondroitin supplement that should help, too."

Megan grinned. "He's already got the warm place. He sleeps on the foot of my bed."

The vet didn't smile in return. "I do have some other concerns." She hesitated, as if searching for the right words. "I think it's wonderful that you're willing to give this old guy a home, and I know you're an experienced dog handler. But I also think he was badly abused, and that could make him aggressive if he feels threatened."

"A *golden retriever?*" Megan stroked Buddy's soft golden fur. "I can't imagine that."

"They're the sweetest dogs on the planet, but people can be unbelievably cruel, and that can change even the kindest of breeds. Maybe this is the wrong dog for you. He could go back to the shelter and you could find a different—"

"No way. Buddy is the right one—I knew it the minute I saw him."

"If you keep him, you'll need to work with him and be very careful…at least until you know him better and can build up his confidence."

Appalled at the vet's subtle insistence, Megan firmly shook her head. "*If* I keep him? Of course I will."

"We've never had a golden growl at us. Cower, balk or tremble, yes. But he growled when we took him back for X-rays."

"Maybe he thought he was being hauled back to dog jail."

"I…think it's more than that. Has he shown any signs of fear or aggression with other strangers? Men, in particular?"

Megan looked up at her. "Good question. Yesterday a friend and I went to an auction, and he had to ride in the backseat of a crew cab pickup. He seemed really wary of Scott at first, and refused to get in."

"Worry over self-preservation and a lack of trust are probably big issues for him right now, so he could be unpredictable and act totally out of character for the breed until he acclimates to home life. You just need to know what you're getting into here. Insurance issues…lawsuits…"

"He was *fearful* of Scott, not belligerent. I can't believe Buddy would harm anyone."

The vet gave her a weary smile. "Well, for your sake, I hope you're right."

Megan pulled to a stop in front of the A-frame cabin, gathered her notebook and a pen, and stepped out to greet the tanned, silver-haired man waiting for her in his bronze BMW M6, the top down.

A soaring wall of glass covering the entire

front of the cabin offered a perfect reflection of the Rockies and dark blue sky. Even without going inside, she knew the property was worth close to a million, maybe even more. The remote location made it a perfect target for the thieves who'd broken in. If the man's car was any clue, they'd probably hauled away a lot of high-end loot.

"Mr. Fairland?"

"Dennis Fairland. Obviously, I own this place." He climbed out of the convertible and glanced impatiently at his watch. "I can only be here a few more minutes. I need to get down to the airstrip in town, so I can make it back to L.A. in time for a dinner meeting at six."

"Have you been inside?"

He shook his head. "I was sailing on Bear Island Lake this morning. Everything was fine when I left. When I got back, the front door was ajar and through the windows I could see that the place had been ransacked."

"Wait here."

The scratched and splintered front door showed obvious signs of forcible entry—probably with a crowbar. She walked around the exterior, looking for any possible clues and checking each window. All of the windows were intact, and she could find nothing on the ground that might have been taken from the house and dropped during a speedy escape.

At the back of the house, a stone path wound through a good acre or more of extensive landscaping—boulders, shrubbery, a graceful trio of aspens and a rainbow of wildflowers. She heard a branch snap somewhere far behind her and turned around, expecting to see that Fairland had followed her after all.

But he was nowhere in sight.

An uneasy feeling prickled at the back of her neck as she scanned the area, sure that she wasn't alone. Could the intruder still be near? Watching?

The underbrush rustled at the far end of the small clearing. Stilled. Just a deer maybe…or a bear spooked by the presence of humans. Then again, maybe not. But why would a thief be foolish enough to linger in the area and risk being seen, with the owner parked out in front and a patrol car here, as well?

She watched. Waited. Nothing else moved.

"Are you done back there?" Fairland

shouted. "I really need to get done with this and be on my way."

Joe Public at his best, she muttered to herself as she continued on her way around the house to the front, where she found him leaning against his car, his arms folded.

"I know you're in a hurry, but I need you to come inside so I can take note of what has been stolen, if you don't mind. Have you called your insurance agent yet?"

Nodding curtly, he pushed away from the car with a grunt of impatience and followed her into the cavernous, cool darkness of the house. "I'll send him the police report, as soon as you have it ready. How soon can it be done?"

"Late this afternoon or tomorrow morning at the latest." She surveyed the beautiful woodwork and slanted pine plank ceilings that soared heavenward.

A fieldstone fireplace nearly filled one wall and rose to the peak high above. Pillowy Italian leather sofas and matching overstuffed chairs were arranged in front of the fireplace, while at the other end of the great room, a heavy crystal vase of flowers topped a dark mahogany dining room table for twelve.

"Remington above the fireplace, gone," he growled.

"Model?"

He made a sound of disgust as he strode through the room. "Original painting, not a rifle. Plus a new fifty-four-inch plasma TV."

She followed him, writing rapidly as he assessed his loss. Silver service for twelve. Several other paintings by lesser artists. Video equipment. In the bedroom, he paused in front of a long, low dresser, then lifted the lid of a jewelry box and sighed. "My wife's jewelry—also gone."

"She left jewelry at a vacation home?"

He made an impatient wave of his hand. "We fly up here often during the summer. So, yes, she brings jewelry when we come and tends to leave it until the end of the season. We aren't skiers, so we close the place up in September."

"Can you give me a list of the pieces and their value?"

His lips curled. "Do you think I'd know that? We have most of it included on an insurance rider, though. She'll have to check on that herself."

"What else was stolen?"

"He missed the professional-level photography equipment I keep in the guest room closet, but he sure found everything else of value," Fairland snarled. He led the way into the next bedroom and opened the closet door, where the camera equipment was clearly visible, then led Megan through the rest of the house. When they were finished, Megan went outside with him on her heels and surveyed the damaged door. "Can you fix this so you'll be able to securely lock up?"

"I called my carpenter while waiting for you to show up. He should be here any minute now."

She smiled at that. "Fast service."

"You get what you pay for—and for the kind of bonus I offered, he should have been here ten minutes ago." Fairland took another look at his watch, then walked a few yards away to punch in a number on his cell phone and barked some orders. He then spun back on his heel and strode to his car. "The guy is just a couple miles away, so I'm leaving."

"Do you trust him?"

The man snorted. "He built the place, and I'm having him add a guest lodge here this summer. He'd hardly jeopardize that contract with petty theft—and everything else of real value is already gone."

"I'll stay until he gets here. I can use the time to lift some fingerprints from the things that were thrown around."

"I can't imagine the sheriff's department up here being well-staffed enough for it to do any good, but be my guest." He climbed behind the wheel and took off in a cloud of dust.

Megan watched him disappear, then settled behind the wheel of the patrol car and started writing more notes for her report. And once again, she felt an uneasy sensation crawl up her neck.

Frowning, she studied the front of the empty house.

In the bright midday sunshine this hardly seemed like a sinister setting, yet it was also two miles up a long, narrow private road that wound through the pines and past massive boulders, offering ample places to hide.

A thief could easily ditch a car along the

way and leave it well hidden while scoping out the place. Wait for the owner to leave… perhaps monitor the man's activities for a few days before making his move.

Even if Fairland had just gone straight to town and back, that would leave ample time to clean the place out, unless the intruder heard something that had scared him off before he could finish. He could still be close by, waiting for a chance to complete his haul. That camera equipment alone was worth thousands.

Megan went inside to lift some fingerprints, and waited until the carpenter arrived. After explaining the situation to him, she headed for her next call at a pizza place on the lake, where the manager suspected an employee was embezzling funds. She had to leave, but she'd be back later—in the evening, after the carpenter was finished.

If someone was still lurking on the property, maybe he'd be back after dark.

And with luck, she might have a chance to catch her suspect at work.

The fingerprints on the beer bottle from Megan's night at the Halfway House Tavern hadn't matched anything in the AFIS computer system.

After she'd checked for Lane's prints and found nothing, she'd searched Montana entries in the NICS—the National Instant Criminal Background Check System using Lane as a first and last name, then looked at the Montana sex offenders registry. No one matched the name Lane, combined with the man's approximate age.

And rare was the person who started a string of serial murders without at least *some* evidence of abnormal behavior or criminal activity beforehand.

Even if he'd given a false name—a definite possibility—the fact that his prints matched nothing in the system indicated that his adult record was clean. Most juvenile records were expunged or sealed...but she would need his correct legal name for a search at any rate.

The business card from Milt Powers, the insurance sales rep, was another matter.

The company had never heard of him.

The address and phone number were false.

And if he'd ever had that e-mail address at the bottom, he sure didn't have it now.

Megan mulled over the possibilities as she sat in her cruiser overlooking the Fairland house from within a stand of pines at one side of the driveway. Creating a false identity and then brazenly sharing it with a young woman in a seedy tavern was hardly the action of someone who had good intentions. He'd wanted to impress her. He'd had the arrogance to expect she'd fall for it. And then he'd likely seen her gravitate toward Lane, which might've made him angry.

Had he been the one who'd followed her home?

On the other hand, Lane had been none too pleasant, in the way he'd forced her into the booth, and it was possible that he'd managed to fly under the radar all these years, without ever coming to the attention of the law....

But those two couldn't possibly be the only suspects she was going to find, though, if she started trolling at the other nightspots the killer's victims had frequented in the months before they died. *Please, God, guide me to the right places, at the right times. Help me find this guy before it's too late.*

Shifting against the back of the seat, she carefully scanned the darkness, listening for any unexpected sounds.

She'd come at dusk, in time to make sure that no one had compromised the new steel door or the windows and to set up a good position.

Now she'd been here over two hours without a hint of activity, and it was time to get back on the road. She'd been so sure...but as shorthanded as the county was, she couldn't stay any longer. Tomorrow, she'd come back out and check the place.

With a sigh, she turned on the ignition and eased out of the trees, then swung wide around a large boulder marking the edge of the man's yard and started for the highway.

It was dark as a tomb out here, the heavy forest blocking any moonlight. Her headlights caught the ever-present wall of trees shouldering close to the tight curves of the lane. Now she had to be getting close to the highway—she could hear a semi gearing down for the sharp grade.

She blinked. Then stared out her windshield.

Had she just seen a glimmer of headlights? Could they be from the highway…or had someone just turned up the lane? This was a private road and the owner was back in California. *No one* should be coming up here this time of night.

In the daylight, she'd seen a lot of places a thief could hide his vehicle along the lane, but along this stretch there was no place to completely pull off the road. There was barely enough space for two vehicles to pass. She dropped her lights to low beam and eased forward, straining to see through the trees.

And suddenly—there it was. A bright swath of light swinging around, and up. Disappearing. And coming around the sharp bend in front of her. *Bingo.*

The oncoming headlights were on bright, blinding her. She slammed to a halt, veering to the narrow shoulder.

The other driver slammed on his brakes. Hesitated.

Then his tires squealed and gravel flew as he launched backward, swerving and slamming against a tree, then pulling forward and into reverse again, in a three-point turn. Her headlights caught the back of his head as he negotiated the sharp bend in the lane. He swung wide and took off, careening down the remaining stretch of road.

It was a black truck.

A black crew cab, the same make and model as Scott's.

A truck that had just expertly executed the fast, efficient kind of turn police officers were trained for from day one and perfected with almost daily use.

She'd never believed in coincidences, yet it just *couldn't* be him. Surely not.

Praying she was right, she flipped on her lights and sirens, negotiated the tight turn ahead, then floored the accelerator and took off after the vehicle ahead. She caught up just as it reached the highway.

The driver burst out onto the highway without stopping. Cranked the wheel and sent the vehicle into a wild sideways slide, fishtailing then nearly spinning off the road.

An earth-shattering semi horn blared. Brakes squealed. The smell of hot rubber spewed into the air as two sets of headlights swung crazily, then faced head-on, just yards apart.

Please, God—please, God, she breathed, her heart jammed in her throat. *Please…*

With barely a yard to spare, the semi swerved. Rocked on its far tires for an eternity. Then slammed back to earth, the cab sliding sideways down the asphalt a good fifty yards before the rig jackknifed and disappeared into the deep ditch on the far side with a terrifying scream of twisting metal.

When she tore her eyes away from the empty highway and looked back, the pickup was gone.

NINE

The truck driver was shaken but apparently unhurt, praise the Lord.

He'd climbed out of his tractor cab by the time Megan made it down the steep embankment and reached the semi with a flashlight. At least fifty and overweight, his hand trembled as he reached for a pack of cigarettes in the breast pocket of his shirt.

"Are you in any pain, sir?"

He ran a hand over his thinning hair. "Bumps and bruises. No blood."

"Chest pain? Difficulty breathing?"

"No. I'm just plain angry at that fool in the pickup who tried to kill me. And look at what happened to my truck." His voice rose. "That's my own rig. It's how I make my living. I'll never forget that man's face. *Never.*"

"I need you to sit quietly until help arrives. Maybe over here—on this log?"

"I need to take a look at my truck first. If—"

"Sir, you need to stay quiet. It's always possible to have internal injuries after something like this, and we don't want to aggravate anything now, do we?"

He grumbled, but finally let her lead him to a place to sit down. She checked his pulse and his pupil dilation—equal, thank goodness—then ordered him to sit still while she hurried up the steep bank to grab some items from her patrol car, leaving the top light bar flashing and doors locked.

Back at his side, she performed another limited assessment. He'd been alert and angry before. Now, his heart rate was faster and his skin felt clammy. In the harsh beam of the flashlight it was hard to tell, but he appeared to be more ashen.

She urged him to lie down on one of the blankets she'd brought from her car and covered him with the other one, after elevating his feet. *Where were the EMTs and others who should be on their way?*

"I need to ask you some questions while we're waiting, sir." She took a quick health history, including his medications and allergies, as much to keep him talking as to gather information for the EMTs in case he lost consciousness before they arrived.

Still, the absolute stillness of the night continued. But wait— Was that the faint sound of a siren? *Please, God, help him get through this. Return him to his family and his job in good health. And protect those who are coming to his aid.*

With all of the deep valleys and steep elevations out here, it could still take a long while for help to arrive. "Well, let's do the accident report, okay?"

He gave a vague wave of his hand, as if to brush away an irritating fly.

"Then you won't need to worry about it later. And that should help you with your insurance claim, too. Okay?"

She got his name—Carl Wilson—and made it through the first few questions when his eyes opened wide in panic and he rolled his head to look at her. "I want that guy found," he rasped in a thready voice. "And I want you to throw the book at him. You hear? Don't…don't let him get…away with this."

"Can you give me a good description of him? Anything—anything at all?"

"Black…hair…" The man's eyes rolled back and his hand fell at his side.

She leaned forward and felt the carotid pulse at the angle of his jaw. *Weak. So weak.*

And once again, she started to pray.

Her eight-to-eight dayshift the next morning came way too soon, after she'd put in hours of overtime at the scene of the accident, then couldn't sleep once she got home.

"So, you had quite a night," Hal said, leaning back in his chair and stacking his hands behind his head. "Any news on the truck driver?"

"I called the hospital around four in the morning. The staff wouldn't tell me anything, but a nurse turned the phone over to Carl's daughter. As I thought, he had internal bleeding. But worse, he suffered a heart attack on the way to the hospital."

"That doesn't sound good." Hal glanced down at the report she'd written. "Older guy.

Obese. Smoker. A lot of stress. He'll be lucky if he pulls through."

"His daughter started crying on the phone. She said his prognosis wasn't good." *His poor family. And him, too—an innocent guy who'd been in the wrong place at the wrong time.*

"You wrote here that he could identify the driver of the black pickup."

"Wilson would've had a ringside view, with his bright headlights and the flat, vertical front of the cab of his semitractor. But he may not remember anything after what he's been through, even if he does manage to survive."

"You saw this guy, too?"

"Just the back of his head—so brief that I can only guess at the driver being male with dark hair. I think it was really suspicious that the guy was heading up to the Fairland place after dark, then took off when he saw me. It was probably the burglar coming back for another haul."

"Any idea who it was?"

"Not yet. But Fairland had to leave, so while I waited for the carpenter to arrive, I lifted prints from a number of items that were thrown around. I'll run them today to see if they match anything in AFIS."

"I'll have Ewan run the prints. He hasn't been half as busy as you."

"Great. Then I'll check on the Fairland place and take a run up to the Halfway House Tavern. I'd like to see if the barkeeper remembers seeing the two guys I ran into that Saturday night."

Hal shuffled through the papers on his desk, then looked at her over his reading glasses. "I actually sent Wes up there last night. I figured you'd want to go back, but decided it would be better if that crew didn't see you in uniform, in case they put two and two together."

Megan blinked. "But…Wes wasn't even there on Saturday night."

"He used the description you put in your report. The bartender definitely remembered 'Milt.' He said snappy dressers and dudes stick out like Angus in fresh snow at that place. He thinks the guy has dropped in a few times, but doesn't remember when and doesn't know his real name. Since it's all cash-only there, there wouldn't be any credit card records. He's probably long gone, though. Thrilling the ladies with his charm and fancy business card somewhere else."

"So that's a dead end for now. Just some guy passing through. What about Lane?"

"That's his real name, actually. Arnold Lane. He's a ranch foreman for the K Bar L ranch. It's right on the county line, about twenty miles straight south of the Halfway House. He's a loner. Single. Known for his temper. But we checked his legal name in the NICS and didn't come up with any priors other than a drunk and disorderly charge, back ten years. Wes is making a run up to the ranch today, to check in on him. And then..." Hal sighed heavily. "Be here in the office at five, because we need to have a meeting. I've gotten a report from the highway patrol about a woman who was held by our suspect, then released with a threatening message."

"What kind of threat?"

"An arrogant promise that the killings aren't going to end. I'm waiting for a fax of the message itself, so we can discuss it later. We've also got to do something about our short-staffing situation, until at least one of the men on leave can come back."

"I thought there wasn't any extra funding."

Hal's short laugh was laden with bitterness. "Funny how serial murders and the threat of lost tourism can loosen the county's purse strings. I think we'll get enough to cover an extra officer maybe three days a week for the next month, and I already have a man in mind."

She lifted her gaze to Hal's, her stomach starting to pitch. "Who?"

"That friend of yours. Scott Anders. I did a little calling yesterday, and he comes with excellent references. We couldn't do any better—especially on such short notice."

"Right," she said faintly. Except for the possibility that Scott—despite her intuition—just may have been involved in the semi crash, and a break-in, to boot. "Have you asked him?"

Hal made an expansive gesture with his hands. "Nope—but I plan to. Great idea, don't you think? And the man has a lot of experience. I'm sure he can teach our department a thing or two while he's at it."

She winced, imagining just how much Scott would have to say to *her*, if he had free rein. "Maybe he won't want a job."

"I'll count on you to help me convince him, then, since you've talked to him more than the rest of us have."

Megan headed to the elementary school to do her annual end of the school year presentation on summer safety awareness, then continued on a long loop through her section of the county.

A domestic disturbance call at the Bufords'—an almost weekly situation.

A call about a dead deer on the highway west of town.

Neighbors feuding over the ownership of an old truck.

All the while, last night's events kept playing through her thoughts. The accident, which might end up taking a man's life. The black pickup.

The way that pickup had slammed backward into a tree when the driver was trying to escape.

The more time she'd spent with Scott, the more foolish she'd felt about ever suspecting him of criminal behavior. He was a good man, with a gentle heart. One who took in damaged animals to simply give them a decent home. A man with a dry sense of humor. Yet…she couldn't let personal feelings interfere—too much was at stake.

And the make, model and color of his truck matched the one she'd seen leaving the Fairland place, while that driver had executed the kind of lightning-fast three-point turn that few people besides law enforcement officers were trained for, and who practiced it. A lot.

She turned around on a side road and headed up into the foothills, sure that she was wrong. Convinced there was no need to even check. Knowing that Scott would probably see through any pretext she came up with to check out his truck. But with lives on the line, how could she not follow every possible avenue?

She turned up the road to his place, half hoping he wouldn't be home.

Jasper bounded out to the mailbox to greet her when she drove in. "So much for wishing," she murmured to herself.

The black pickup was by the tractor he'd found at the auction, and from behind the barn, in the vicinity of Attila's corral, came the sound of pounding.

She parked behind the pickup and got out, carefully surveying the tailgate and rear fenders for any evidence of damage. From the sound of the impact last night, it should show fresh dents and the gleam of newly damaged metal. Instead, she could see only an assortment of nicks and scrapes, none of which appeared to be new. *Thank you, Lord.*

"Looking for something?"

She jumped, startled at the sound of his voice so close by. Heat rushed to her face. "I was out and about, and thought I'd stop in and say hi. I…um…didn't mean to be nosy, but I…noticed your truck has some scratches and chips. Might want to get those fixed this summer, before winter snow. The salt on the highways is tough on vehicles, believe me."

"I'll be sure to keep that in mind," he said dryly, fixing her with a knowing look. "Anything else?"

She glanced at the hammer in his hand. "I take it you have the goat here now?"

His expression softened. "I hired a guy with a trailer, and he brought them all over. The goat is closed in a box stall until I can reinforce his fence. The goose is around here somewhere… probably chasing the barn cats."

"And the pony?"

"He's in with Attila, and I think they're new best friends. Good thing, because the pony needs a guide."

"Guide?"

"He's blind."

Her heart melted. "Poor guy."

"He's actually doing really well. Their enclosure is free of obstacles, and he just hangs close to Attila's flanks to get around, or listens for where his buddy is."

She looked up into depths of kindness in Scott's light blue eyes. "You really are one very cool guy."

He reached up and touched her cheek. Just a featherlight, brief touch, but it sent a delicate jolt clear through her, then settled around her heart.

"I…" He hesitated, and cleared his throat before continuing, the flash of tenderness in his voice gone. "Good luck with your case. If that's all, then I'd better get back to work here."

"Right. And…I've got to run, too. See you later."

Waving her fingertips, she climbed into the patrol car and drove away, feeling an uncomfortable sense of guilt.

She'd *had* to check his truck, just to make sure. Even if he'd been nothing but kind and thoughtful, to the point of trying to protect her back at the tavern, nothing could stand in the way of being thorough…and definitely not her personal feelings.

Her cell phone rang.

She negotiated a tight turn out onto the county road, then picked it up to check the screen, half expecting to see Scott's name. But it was an unfamiliar number.

Frowning, she pulled over to the side of the road, punched a button on the phone and lifted it to her ear. All her work-related calls came through the county dispatcher. She never gave out her private number…so who could it be?

"Just as I thought," a man growled. The note of satisfaction in his voice made her shiver. "You had to go see your 'friend' because you had to check on him, just in case. Sad isn't it, finding you can't fully trust even the people you know?"

"I don't know what you mean."

He ignored her. "You had to see if the

truck was his, didn't you? I knew you would, because I know you very well."

"Who is this?"

She blinked, then pulled the phone away from her ear and took another look at the number on the screen. He sounded eerily familiar, yet not—as if he were trying to mask his voice through a heavy layer of cotton. Had she overheard him in the crowded tavern? At the auction, or on the streets of Copper Cliff… or sometime in the past?

Perhaps she'd even arrested him—which could account for the edge in his voice.

"Maybe…we could meet somewhere. You could tell me what this is all about."

He swore under his breath. "Don't play games with me. You won't like my rules."

"Who is this?"

"Ahh. Perhaps I'll let you find out. Perhaps not. Let's just see how good you *really* are at your job. So long, sweetheart."

"Wait. Talk to me—"

"Later," he whispered. "You'll like it, I promise."

And then the connection went dead.

* * *

Megan stared out the window of the cruiser, sorting through her thoughts. Even now she felt a chill that had nothing to do with the weather.

The caller had figured that she'd drive up to Scott's to look for damage on his truck. He *knew* she had done so. Of even more interest, he'd called her within minutes after she left Scott's place. Had he tailed her on the highway and watched her head in this direction? Or had he been hiding somewhere close by?

Maybe he'd seen her with Scott sometime on Sunday, then had driven his own black truck last night, hoping that anyone who spotted him near the Fairland place would assume Scott was behind the wheel.

But if so, it made no sense for him to call and taunt her about it. An intelligent suspect—though granted, the label was an oxymoron more often than not—would simply drop out of sight.

She called Elaine, the day-shift dispatcher, and asked her to run the caller's phone number, plus any Montana registrations for a black 2003 Ford F-350 crew cab pickup, then headed for the Fairland property to make sure there hadn't been a break-in after she left.

Elaine called back within minutes. "I checked with the DMV. There's just one of those vehicles registered in Marshall County, to a Scott Anders here in town. Statewide, there's over two hundred in that year, model and color, but none in the neighboring counties."

"Put out a county-wide bulletin on that model, especially one with any sort of rear damage. But see if you can get the plates on the Anders vehicle and exclude that one. I've already checked it out."

"Got it." She paused for a long moment. "I have bad news on that phone number. It's for one of those cheap, prepaid cell phones that you can buy with cash at a discount store. There's no way to track it. Buyers can activate them online by just punching in a zip code."

Which of course could be false.

"Thanks. I figured as much."

So the anonymous caller wasn't entirely stupid—she could give him that much. Yet why would he taunt her about the truck?

Unless he had another agenda.

One far more dangerous, and he was getting his jollies by inviting her to play. Her heart picked up a faster beat as she drove.

She'd play, all right, but he'd soon discover his mistake in taking that chance.

Because his days of freedom were numbered.

TEN

A couple of traffic stops slowed her down, but Megan finally reached the Fairland place at three o'clock.

She half expected to see windows broken and the new door wide-open, but as she stepped out of her car, the door appeared to be shut tight and the pristine expanse of westward-facing glass gleamed in the midday sun.

A folded yellow sheet of paper was fluttering on the door. Not a good thing to leave there if it was a dated invoice from the carpenter, given how long Fairland would be gone.

"Nothing like letting the bad guys know he's not home," she muttered under her breath as she strode up to the door.

The door threshold would be too tight to slide the paper inside, but she could at least put it in an envelope and mail it to him here, because surely he had his mail held while he was gone.

She reached for it, then froze. It wasn't an invoice from the carpenter. Her name was written on it in an elegant computer font. But no one should have expected that she'd have any reason to be here today.

She turned slowly, surveying the property for any suspicious movement. Anything that might have been disturbed since she was here last. Then she slid a fingernail through the cellophane tape seal and opened it wide.

Again, the fancy, swooping font.

So you are here. I thought as much. You really are so predictable.

The amusing thing is, I am not…and you will have to jump at my bidding. I'm so glad there will now be an element of fun.

Happy hunting, my dear.

My own hunt will be successful if yours is not.

She fought the urge to rip the paper in a thousand shreds, and instead held it by the narrowest possible edge to avoid contaminating it with her own fingerprints as she strode to the patrol car.

Once inside, she gently stored the letter in a manila folder. But even with it stowed safely at her side, the words played through her thoughts a hundred times over as she headed straight back to town.

It was a threat.

A taunt.

A promise.

And it was directed at her.

Hal instructed Betty to hold all calls, then firmly shut the door of his office and sat down behind his desk. With all four deputies there, the walls seemed to press in from all sides. "So what do you have for me?"

Ewan ran a hand over his thinning hair. "Not much. I ran the prints from the Fairland house and came up with nothing. They all matched the owner or one other person, consistently. Neither one had any history."

"Fairland's wife is usually there with him, and the second set was hers," Megan said. "The intruder likely wore gloves, because he *had* to have handled the furniture and other items that he tossed around. But that's no surprise. Anyone with a TV can watch the

CSI reruns and learn the benefit of wearing gloves."

Ewan nodded. "Our serial killer learned *that* lesson all too well."

"Well, I drove up to the K Bar L and took a look around," Wes said. "Lane was gone. The owner wasn't there, but the ranch hands said Lane left early this morning to haul a load of cattle up to Billings, but he'd be back tonight." He hitched a shoulder. "I didn't get much, really. The guy has worked there for about two years. Stays to himself most of the time, doesn't have much to say. One of the hands said he takes off now and then and is gone for a few days. Lane has told them that he goes to visit his sister in Rawlins and maybe that's true, but no one has ever seen her."

Hal looked up from the tablet on his desk, where he'd been jotting notes. "Did you get her name?"

"Yep, Barbara Lane. But I haven't had a chance yet to do a search for her address and phone number."

Hal flipped his pen between his fingers. "Megan."

She quickly summarized last night's

encounter with the black pickup and the accident, then took a deep breath. "Carl Wilson—the truck driver—swore he could I.D. the man behind the wheel of the pickup. Only now, he's in bad shape at the hospital and might not pull through."

"But we're just talking about a break and enter here, really," Ewan interjected in a bored tone. "Proving who the driver of the pickup was, without physical evidence, would be a hard sell in court—even if this ends up as vehicular homicide. Anyway, I thought we were concerned with bigger issues right now."

"That's a big one in my book." Megan glanced around the room. "The truck I saw last night slammed backward into a tree, and it hit *hard*. I went to check out a similar black pickup in town, but it had no damage on the rear fender or bumper. The interesting thing is that just minutes after checking the truck, I got a call on my personal cell phone. Anonymous. Untraceable. The caller gloated about how he *knew* I'd be going up to check out Scott Anders's truck. Then he taunted me about whether or not I'd ever figure out who he was."

All four pairs of eyes in the room were riveted on her now.

"He also delivered a subtle threat. Something about talking to me later, and that I'd really like it." She made a face of disgust. "He sounded smarmy and overconfident. But it gets even *more* interesting."

She lifted a manila folder from her lap and handed it to Hal. "I got this. I went out to double-check the Fairland property, guessing that the intruder may have returned during the night. This note was taped to the door. I already tried to lift prints from it, but there wasn't anything legible."

Hal studied it, his face grim. Then he passed the folder around the room. "It could be a copycat. Someone who wants to play into all the gossip about the Full Moon murders, just for kicks."

"I don't think so." She stood and paced to the window, then turned back to face everyone. "I think our suspect *was* at that tavern. Maybe not anyone I talked to, but I think he took the bait. Someone followed me home—too far back for me to be sure, but I heard a vehicle come into my driveway right after I got there. I think he saw my patrol car parked by the house that night, or figured it out later, and now he wants to play games. Maybe he even broke into the Fairland place knowing it's in the area I cover."

"To draw you away from town and put you in a more vulnerable position? Or prove that he can manipulate you?" Jim frowned. "I don't like this at all."

"Well, I can't stop doing my job. I think he's going to up the stakes and try to prove we can't catch him. But if we don't, a lot more people are going to die."

"But why did he target you?" Wes asked slowly.

"Maybe he figures I'll be frightened and weak because I'm a woman. Maybe he figures it will be more exciting if he dares me to catch him. A male superiority thing."

Hal's shoulders sagged. "We won't have long to wait. He's already working on his next move. The highway patrol found a woman staggering along the highway between here and Battle Creek, early this morning. Half-dressed, her hands bound with duct tape. Beat up pretty bad, but at least she was alive. She said it was dark and he wore a mask, so she never got a good look at his face."

Megan closed her eyes for a moment. "Raped?"

"No. But she was carrying a message." Hal blew out a long breath as he leaned over his desk and motioned for Megan to take it. "I received this copy by fax. Look familiar?"

She stared at it, then looked up at him, feeling the blood drain from her face as she read it. *This one goes free—but the next won't be so lucky.* "This font is an exact match of the note left on Fairland's door. So I was right."

He nodded. "And now, we need to get to work."

"The suspect has to know that the truck driver saw his face. That means Wilson is in danger."

"Jim, get over to the hospital and alert them to the situation. See if you can get any information on the man's condition, even if you have to track down his relatives to do it. Wes, work on tracking down Lane's sister. And, Megan, you stay here. You can start calling every roadhouse in the county. I want you to describe the guy who called himself Milt, and see if anyone else has seen him around."

"So you want me to ride a desk. Stay here, when I could be out doing a lot more."

Hal glared at her. "Someone has to do it. Might as well be you."

"You know our suspect could be someone we haven't even thought of yet."

"True."

"There's almost two dozen little towns in this county with a couple hundred people or less. Any one of those wide spots in the road could be harboring the killer."

"True."

"So without every possible officer out in the field, we don't stand a chance."

"Oh, yes we do. Because there's a good chance he'll surface again and try to lure you out, wanting you to play his game. And if that time comes, we'll be ready. I promise you that."

ELEVEN

After hours of sitting at a desk in the Marshall County Sheriff's office, looking up the phone numbers of bars and taverns in the Internet yellow pages, then calling every last one of them with a description of Milt Powers, Megan knew two things.

Milt had apparently appeared out of thin air when he showed up at the Halfway House Tavern, because no one else had ever seen him, so maybe he *had* been just passing through.

And the last thing she'd ever want was to be tied to a desk as a county sheriff.

At eight o'clock, three hours after the sheriff and secretary had gone home, she sighed heavily, shut down the computer, grabbed her keys and cell phone, and headed out to her patrol car. The phone vibrated in her hand, sending her heart into overdrive as she lifted it to check the screen.

A sense of relief washed through her. "Scott. What's up?"

"I left you a couple messages. You're a hard lady to catch."

"I had to finish out my shift in the office this evening, so I had the ringer off."

His laughter was low and warm. "Why does that sound as if you were put on a time-out?"

"I was. Sort of." She found herself smiling. "Not that I did anything wrong."

"That's what they all say. There's never a guilty person on death row."

"Or in a jail cell, for that matter."

"Hey, Jasper and I were thinking this evening, and well, it seemed awfully quiet at home. I suggested that we run into town for pizza and he agreed—but now I've just picked up this hot, fresh, steaming pizza absolutely loaded with chicken, fresh parmesan and some sort of garlic-ranch sauce. And it's just way too big."

"You must have gone to Gino's. They have the most incredible Chicken Ranch Pizza I've ever tasted. You could always save the rest for tomorrow."

"Or we could share it. What do you think, are you hungry at all? This thing is *huge*. Maybe we could meet in the town square at one of the picnic tables?"

"Well..."

"You may be thinking no, but I'll bet your stomach is saying *yes*." He fell silent for a moment. "Wait—what about your dog? I suppose you do have to go home."

He'd handed her an easy excuse.

She could head home and keep her life as uncomplicated as it had been for the past couple of years, no questions asked. But suddenly that option wasn't appealing at all.

"Actually, the previous property owner installed a swinging pet entrance in the kitchen door. Buddy figured it out the second day."

"So you'll meet me?"

"Honestly, that pizza sounds like an offer too good to refuse."

During the summer, the little park was often filled with tourists, and arts and crafts booths lined the perimeter. An assortment of musicians played for the dollars thrown in their empty guitar cases on the ground.

Now, the benches and picnic tables were all empty, and the only other people were an elderly couple walking their beagle, and a group of high school kids shooting baskets on the tennis court that also boasted a hoop.

Scott had already arrived, and was leaning against a picnic table with Jasper sitting at his feet. "You came," he said, the laugh lines at the corners of his eyes deepening. "I was afraid you'd change your mind and leave me with all this food."

She smiled back, her mood lifting at simply seeing him there. "Not when Gino's pizza is involved."

He turned and shook out a folded scarlet tablecloth, letting the breeze catch it so it drifted down on the picnic table.

She laughed. "Wow. You're good."

"I worked my way through college at a restaurant. Basic Life Skills 101, for a kid who grew up with paper plates and boxed mac and cheese."

From a grocery sack he withdrew napkins and bottles of cold water, then he lifted the pizza box from one of the benches. "Still hot."

They sat down opposite one another, each lifting a fragrant slice gooey with rich, heavy cheese.

"Did you have a good day catching bad guys?"

"Always."

"So what made you decide on law enforcement?"

She took a second bite of pizza and closed her eyes, savoring each subtle nuance of the fresh herbs. "I wanted to go after those bad guys, not worry about them coming after me."

"Sounds like a good reason."

"So what about you? I know you're on a medical leave…but I'm curious about why you came this far west and actually bought property. Seems permanent to me."

"It is. I inherited some money years ago from my grandmother. I invested it in the stock market. Built it up, took a big hit when the market fell, worked to build it up again, and…" He gave a wry laugh. "Well, the market fell again. I finally decided to invest it in property and do what I'd always wanted to do. So here I am, in the mountains."

Jasper had been eyeing Scott, his tail wagging. Now, he moved over to stare at Megan. She broke off a bit of crust and tossed it to him. "So…what are your plans? The place you bought isn't big enough for an operational ranch. Are you thinking about a dude ranch? A rustic resort?"

"Maybe the latter, someday. I've got twenty acres, with a number of sites that have stunning views of the mountains. Perfect places for a scattering of secluded cabins, for the people who don't want to feel like they're in a village or crowded resort."

"Sounds perfect."

"I think so. It could be a nice supplemental income to go along with the writing."

"Cool. So what do you write?"

"I've done a lot of articles for magazines over the years. Now, I've also started back to work on a suspense novel that's been on the back burner for a while."

"*Really* cool." She thought for a moment. "So that's why you don't get to town much."

"Nope. I'm pretty much a hermit, most of

the time." He gave a self-deprecating laugh. "I'm safer there, anyway. When I do go to town I somehow end up bringing home another animal or two—sort of like your friend with the animal shelter, only my residents never move on."

He really was a fascinating man, despite everything.

He'd been a cop, so he ought to know better…yet, like Prince Charming in some fairy tale, he'd already insisted on coming to her rescue twice—from the mayor's sharp remarks and Lane, the aggressive man at the tavern.

She didn't want or need rescuing. That was *her* job, as a county deputy. Yet that charming twinkle in his eyes did the funniest things to her heart.

But charming twinkles aside, she'd long since accepted that God didn't have marital bliss on His agenda for her life, because she'd been down this road before and it always led to dead ends well before any talk of happily-ever-afters.

It would be so easy to set all logic aside and fall for Scott anyway. To take that risk just one more time. He seemed to be everything she'd ever imagined about the kind of man she'd like to meet, and more. Intelligent. Witty. Honorable. A strong protector with a good and loving heart, if his growing menagerie was any clue. She hadn't even known him that long, yet just the brush of his hand against hers made her heart start doing crazy little flip-flops in her chest…as if there were some innate, chemical reaction going on.

But even if he'd been a cop, there was no guarantee that she wouldn't face another painful heartbreak if she risked her emotions once again, and that had happened one too many times already. The giddy, silly feelings dancing around her heart, urging her to take the chance, were as fickle as the Montana sun in January.

Solid relationships were tough for someone in law enforcement. Long, late hours, the stress and the fears, the issues of trust…and it wasn't just her. Maybe Hal enjoyed a solid marriage, but hadn't all of the other deputies been through a divorce at least once?

No matter what her foolish heart wanted, she would be leaving Scott Anders alone.

"Hey, there," he said, studying her with concern. "Something wrong?"

Jerked back into the present, she felt a blush warm the back of her neck. *Nothing, as long as I always play it safe.* "Sorry—just thinking." She pinned on a bright smile. "I really appreciate your invitation. This is perfect, after a long day. Great pizza, a beautiful spot outdoors."

"Don't forget the good company."

Despite her every intention, she still couldn't resist the chance to flirt…just a little. What could be the harm? "That's right," she said with a laugh. "Jasper is a *great* dog."

He gave her a pained look. "Wait a minute. *He* didn't bring you pizza."

"Nope. But he's awfully sweet, anyway." From the corner of her eye she caught a glimpse of Hal striding across the lawn. "Oh-oh."

Scott followed the direction of her gaze. "What—are you playing hooky?"

"I…was supposed to talk you into something." She studied him over the slice of pizza in her hand. "Not that I expected it would happen."

"What—a confession?" He drawled, his intent gaze fixed on hers.

"Howdy," Hal called out. "Have you two had a good visit?"

Megan looked between the two men. "Not… yet."

Hal clapped Scott on the shoulder. "I suppose she told you how short-staffed we are?"

A corner of Scott's mouth twitched. "At length, actually."

Megan stiffened. "That isn't exactly true."

Turning to Hal, Scott ignored her. "I just hope your department is back up to full staffing soon, so your officers don't need to take any unnecessary risks."

She bristled. "I don't take chances that could jeopardize an investigation, Anders."

"What about your personal safety?"

Hal frowned as he glanced between them, not quite picking up on the undertones. "Have you ever thought of working part-time while you're up in this area, Anders?"

"Nope."

"Not even law enforcement—if you had the chance?"

"Make that a *definite* no."

"You're sure?"

"Right now my gun arm wouldn't pass muster. But I've left all of that behind in any case. For good."

"Want to work for just a few months?"

"I'm not your man."

Hal gave him a good-ole-boy clap on his back. "I'll tell you what. Give us just a single month. See how you like it."

"Thanks for the offer, but I'm just not interested." Scott shrugged. "Anyway, I think working here would play havoc with my current medical leave."

"We're talking consultant time. A few days a week…without any twelve-hour shifts of patrol time behind the wheel."

Scott fell silent at that, and Hal quickly pressed his point. "All we'd need is a month or so. We've got three men out, and we could use a good investigator. Just help us with this murder case. Keep your own time card, your own hours."

At that, Scott laughed. "You must've talked to my old boss."

Hal grinned in return. "I did hear about

your fourteen-plus-hour days when you were on a tough case back home, but that's not what I'm after here. We need any help we can get. But to bring in someone with your expertise, we'd be even more grateful."

Scott sighed. "Well…"

"Short-term. Change your mind, and you can quit. No hard feelings."

"I'll agree to a strict consultant basis, for assisting with the current murder investigation." Scott leveled a look at Megan. "And also as backup if needed—so your officers will be safer."

Megan stared at him, horrified, as the implications grew clear. He was planning on watching over her. Getting in the way of what she needed to do, out of some misguided chivalrous code. "I think that's a bad idea. We just need someone to take over twelve-hour shifts that aren't being covered right now."

Hal chuckled. "Actually, I think this is just about perfect. Anders, I'll talk to the county supervisors first thing tomorrow about the pay, and how we can handle the personnel details. With luck, we can have you on board in no time."

* * *

At the sharp rap on the door frame leading to the deputy's shared office area, Megan looked up, thankful for the interruption after working on the computer all morning. "Heading out for your lunch break, Betty?"

The gray-haired woman shook her head as she handed over a pink phone message slip. "We just got a call. Arnold Lane never showed up last night at the ranch. He was driving the ranch semi, and the owner is really concerned. I tried calling the sheriff but he isn't answering his cell."

"Have you talked to the highway patrol?"

"I just called them. No accident reports have come in on any semis within the last twenty-four hours. No traffic stops on a truck with that license plate, either."

"So maybe the man was too tired to drive all the way back, and just took a nap somewhere. Or he checked into a motel."

"The owner of the ranch doesn't think so. Lane has made the same trip dozens of times and is always back before dark. The ranch hands told him that a deputy was out there yesterday asking questions about Lane, and now he's concerned." She pulled a face. "And that's putting it mildly. This is one unpleasant man."

The Halfway House Tavern was fifty-six miles away, and the ranch was twenty miles south of that. It couldn't be farther from the sheriff's office and still be in the same county, and a trip there would take the whole afternoon. But that was infinitely more appealing than being cooped up in the sheriff's office doing busy work.

"Where is Hal, do you know?"

Betty's face filled with concern. "At one of his wife's doctor's appointments. He tries to be with her every time, you know. That's probably why his phone is off."

"Then I'll follow up on this. Everyone else is busy."

"But—"

"Just let him know when he comes back in."

"Wait—he said you have to take Scott along if you go out on something like this. Remember?"

"I've been in this job for a lot of years, Betty. I can handle it."

She pursed her lips. “It isn’t about you. Hal wants the new guy acclimated to what’s going on. He was adamant about it—he told me himself.”

Megan hesitated, then sighed. “I’ll call Scott and see if he’s available. If not, then I can at least say I tried.”

Already feeling the adrenaline flowing back into her veins, Megan grabbed her service belt and keys and headed out the door.

Sam Fillmore, owner of the K Bar L, met Megan and Scott at the door of his sprawling, hacienda-style home. Scott stood back and let Megan take the lead.

“Second time in two days that the law has been here,” Fillmore growled. “And now my foreman, semi and a sale barn check for a load of cattle are missing. Mind telling me what’s going on?”

From the massive ranch sign hanging above the ranch road to the well-kept barns and fences, he appeared to be a successful rancher, but his face was heavily lined and weathered to an ageless, almost mummified state of preservation, and his mouth appeared set in a permanent scowl.

"You still haven't heard from him, then," Megan said.

He swore under his breath. "If I had, I wouldn't have called the sheriff, and you wouldn't be standing here."

Megan had told Scott about Betty's low opinion of Sam Fillmore on the long drive out here, and the older woman's assessment was right on.

"I checked with the highway patrol just a few minutes ago, and they've put out a bulletin on your truck," Megan continued. "None of the patrolmen remember seeing it in the last day or so, and your K Bar L logo is certainly memorable. I've seen it in the past and you can't miss the white-on-red design."

"Why did that other deputy come out yesterday to ask about Lane before he even disappeared?"

"To ask him a few questions, but maybe I could ask you a couple more and save us all a third trip. I understand Lane has a sister in Rawlins. Have you met her?"

Fillmore snorted. “He doesn’t have a sister. No family at all, far as I know.”

Megan looked up at him sharply. “You’re sure?”

“That’s what he wrote on his application form for next of kin when I hired him. Why would he lie?”

To make himself harder to trace? “Good question, sir,” Scott said. “Did he have references when he came here?”

“Sure. A couple of cattle ranches in the Sand Hills of western Nebraska. A horse ranch in southern Colorado. I called ’em all.”

Megan tapped her pen against her clipboard. “Do you have those numbers in a file somewhere?”

“This ain’t some big corporation, ma’am. Somebody gits hired, they work hard, and they stay. If they don’t work out, they’re gone. I don’t need to keep some fancy file on everyone. Simple, but it works.”

“So he’s been a good, dependable employee. What about friends? Enemies?”

“He don’t even hang out with the other ranch [illegible]ds, much less anyone else. And I don’t pry [illegible]ersonal business.”

"If he shows up so I can ask him some questions, he'll give me straight answers?"

"I expect so. Like I said, if he was a troublemaker, he'd a been outta here already." Fillmore's gaze flickered. "But I can't rightly say where he goes or what he does on his time off. If you find out anything bad, I want to know. I can't afford to keep someone on I can't trust."

After jotting down a few notes, she looked up at Scott. "Anything you want to add?"

"What about gambling? Do you know if Lane has any heavy debts?"

Fillmore shook his head.

"Alcohol? Drugs?"

"If he was an alcoholic or used drugs and I caught him, he would've been tossed off the ranch on his ear," the rancher snapped.

Scott ignored the man's surly tone. "What about new friends? Anyone who started hanging around or calling? More mail than usual, boxes being delivered? Any unusual travel recently?"

"Nada. Look, if the guy has disappeared, there's nothing I can do about that. Far as I'm concerned, he's already fired. The sales barn stopped my missing check, but I want that semi back…and I want it back in one piece."

"If it turns up, you'll be the first to know." Her mouth compressed in a firm line and her voice flinty, Megan handed him her business card. "Contact us if you learn anything, as well. I can assure you that we want to solve this as much as you do."

"Really." The rancher's voice dripped acid. "When you've got a forty-thousand-dollar rig missing, then maybe I'll believe you."

"That man is obnoxious." Megan fumed on the way back to Copper Cliff. "I'm surprised anyone would ever want to work with him."

Scott looked over at her, amused. "Makes me wonder how long any of his ranch hands stay. The ones who do might well band together…sort of an 'us against the boss' camaraderie."

She glanced over at him, then turned her attention back to the stretch of empty highway ahead. "Since Lane went missing right after Wes had stopped out at the ranch to ask about him, maybe the other hands alerted him to stay away?"

"Though that begs the question of how he could imagine that he could lie low for any length of time with a fire-engine-red rig emblazoned with K Bar L on the side. It doesn't make sense…unless he'd stashed a personal vehicle somewhere, or had friends he could count on."

"Good point." Megan picked up the mike and radioed Elaine. "I need you to check on any vehicles registered to Arnold Lane."

In seconds Elaine was back on the radio. "Red '82 Chevy pickup. Montana plates."

Scott grabbed a slip of paper from a tablet affixed to the dash and wrote down the license plate number.

"Put out an alert on the vehicle, will you?" Megan added. "Let me know what you hear."

Then she picked up her cell phone and punched the speed dial for Wes. He answered on the third ring. "Hey, you were going to check on Barbara Lane, down in Rawlins. Any luck?"

"I found over fifty Lanes in Montana. None live in Rawlins. I've been able to talk to forty-three of them already, and the others are either too elderly or have recently deceased."

"So did you come up with anything?"

"None of the women I talked to had even heard of Arnold Lane, or the K Bar L Ranch."

"I was afraid of that. It confirms what his boss just told me." Megan disconnected the call. "But why would Lane lie? What's the point?"

"He could have some woman he's been seeing…or maybe he goes off drinking. Or it could be something much worse…which is looking more likely all the time."

"I don't know what this guy is up to, but whatever it is, he definitely has something to hide." She bit her lower lip. "Once you start adding things up, he could even be our Full Moon Killer."

"If he is, we've got about fifteen days before the next full moon to find him, and he already knows that we're on his tail."

She nodded. "This state has more wilderness than we could ever cover. If we do find him in time, it will only be through the grace of God."

TWELVE

Back in Copper Cliff, Megan took a detour and pulled to a stop in front of the Marshall County regional hospital. At just fifty beds, the L-shaped, one-story brick building held a thirty-bed long-term care unit, a ten-bed skilled unit and ten hospital beds, though the more critical cases were airlifted to Billings or Bozeman.

She said a silent prayer before she walked inside and stopped at the front desk. “Is Carl Wilson still here?”

The receptionist looked up from her computer. “Hi, Officer. He is, but—” She hit a few keys and studied the monitor. “This says he is to receive no visitors.”

“Is he worse?”

She smiled. “We can’t release information. You know that.”

"I'm not exactly a visitor. I'd need to talk to him, if he's able."

The receptionist's smile slipped. "I really can't let you go back there. You could talk to the nurse, though. Or his daughter, if she's still here. She might've slipped out for a bite to eat. Just hold on, and I'll page the unit."

"This is important."

The woman picked up the phone, spoke to someone, then waved Megan toward the north wing. "Stop at the nurse's station."

Nodding her thanks, Megan strode to the nurse's station, where a middle-aged nurse stood behind the desk. "I hear you want to talk to Carl, but I'm afraid he's in no shape to visit."

"I know he was in a coma when he arrived Sunday night, and that he'd had a heart attack en route. So there's no change?"

"You aren't actually a relative…" The nurse smiled apologetically.

"But I am."

Megan turned and found a woman standing at the open door of a lounge. "You must be his daughter."

She stepped forward with a strained smile. "Mona Wilson. Can I help you?"

"I'm so sorry about the accident. How are you holding up?"

Her dark brown eyes sheened with tears. "Not so good, I guess. I'm really worried about him because he isn't showing any signs of improvement."

"Has he been conscious at all?"

She shook her head. "He's breathing on his own, thank goodness. But he hasn't opened his eyes or spoken. H-he's got tubes and wires everywhere."

"Since they're keeping him here, that must be a good sign."

She hesitated, then nodded. "I sit with him almost all the time, talking to him and hoping that he'll wake up."

"I'm sure he knows you're here."

"I—I think so. I feel so bad, though—I've got to leave in a few minutes and can't be here all weekend." A tear spilled down her cheek. "My daughter is coming home from a week with her father. I have to meet her plane, then get her set up and drive her to cheerleading camp."

"The doctors and nurses will be only a phone call away, though." Megan looked up at the nurse. "Right?"

"Absolutely. Your father has been stable. We'll hope and pray that he does just fine while you're away."

Megan rested a comforting hand on Mona's arm. "There's one thing you can do for me when he does wake up."

"Anything. If you hadn't been there, he might've stayed down in that ditch all night. He could've died."

"I have to be honest, though. If I hadn't been in the area, the guy who drove him off the road might not have driven so erratically. He took one look at my patrol car and raced off."

"Then he had to be guilty of something, even before the accident."

"I'd really like to get him. There'll be insurance and legal issues later, and if we can identify the guy it could be of financial benefit for your father."

"B-but what can I do?"

"Before he passed out at the scene, he told me he would never forget the face of the man in the pickup. Call me right away when he starts talking, okay?" Megan handed her a business card. "With all he's been through he may not remember anything at all. But I hope so, because the man I'm looking for may be responsible for some other...problems in the area."

"Leave a card with the nurses, too. If Dad wakes up and there's a chance he can describe the monster that did this to him and drove away, I want to make *sure* you get the message."

Scott drove into Megan's driveway and pulled to a stop next to her patrol car, then rested his wrists on the top of the steering wheel and studied the cabin.

On their long trip back to town from the Fillmore ranch, one topic had led to another. He'd somehow finagled a dinner invitation, though second thoughts about accepting it had been swirling through his mind since he'd left home. But now, he could see welcoming, soft light glowing through the open windows. And even from here, he could smell the aroma of something wonderful. Pie? Could it actually be *peach* pie?

But it wasn't the prospect of a home-cooked meal that had brought him here. It was the woman herself. And that fact had warning bells clanging in his head.

What was he thinking? He'd left the police department and the rest of his tumultuous old life behind with a move halfway across the country, and he'd finally found a measure of peace. So what was he doing here—repeating past mistakes?

If nothing else, Olivia's defection had taught him the value of being completely alone.

Jasper stared at him from the opposite side of the front seat and whined.

"You think it's a mistake, too?"

The dog looked out the window and whined louder.

Now Scott saw the reason—Megan's golden retriever was sitting in the shadows of the porch. The old dog woofed and Jasper answered with a series of eager barks.

"Traitor." Resigned, Scott opened the door and Jasper bounded out after him to race up the stairs and sniff noses with his new pal.

Megan appeared at the door a moment later, a voluminous white apron wrapped around her trim waist and a set of oven mitts on her hands. "Sometimes Buddy just sits out here at night and barks when the bats swoop by, but I *thought* I heard something different. Welcome."

Her auburn hair was lit to a gold-edged nimbus by the light behind her, her voice was low and warm and inviting. And just like that, his doubts melted away. "I found you with Google Maps on the computer…sort of. Things got a little sketchy in the dark, though, once I got out in the country."

"Everyone has trouble. It's not the map program's fault, it's that the numbering system out here is a little wonky. And one of the roads got washed out last year but was never replaced. I hope you're hungry."

"More so by the minute. Something sure smells wonderful." He walked up the steps to the broad covered porch. She'd set up a table out here, with a pair of flickering candles smelling of cinnamon and a bouquet of wildflowers in an old blue canning jar. A pair of faceted water glasses sparkled in the candlelight. "And this looks beautiful."

"I don't entertain very often. You'll have to forgive my china—I have just a partial set of my grandmother's so it doesn't all match."

He laughed at that. "I'm glad you haven't seen my kitchen, then."

She disappeared into the house and brought out pitchers of raspberry iced tea and lemonade.

"Let me help carry."

"Nah, just pour. Tea for me, but I made both just in case. I'll be right back."

She returned in a few minutes with a big wooden bowl of raspberry and almond spinach salad. "I didn't even think to ask you what you like. Please, don't hesitate to turn anything down." She looked up at him and grinned. "So have a seat. I'll only be offended if you try to suffer in silence."

He watched her serve the salad with deep pleasure. "Well, the first course is definitely a work of art."

She took a seat across from him. "Thanks. I—"

From somewhere in the cabin came the

sound of her cell phone. "I'm sorry. I should probably get that."

She returned a minute later, her face pale. "This is awful. I hate to do this—but I think I need to make a quick run into town."

"Trouble?"

She tipped her head in acknowledgment. "You probably read in the paper about the semi accident, and the old fellow who was hurt. His daughter just called."

"The paper said he was in a coma."

"There are also some…other issues, so the hospital has been on alert to watch for any unexpected visitors. Someone snuck into his room earlier tonight, then disappeared before security arrived. They notified the daughter and now she's in a panic because she's out of town for a few days and can't check on him."

"She can't talk to the nurses?"

"She already did." Megan's mouth tipped in a wry smile. "But she's really worried anyway."

"I'll go with you."

"You don't have to. If you want to stay and

eat your salad and just relax, I'll be back in twenty minutes."

He stood, taking in the concern in her eyes, and gave her a quick hug. "You went to a lot of work, so we should enjoy this meal together. We can take my truck, if you want to."

"We'd better take my patrol car. Though after twelve hours in it today, I'd hoped it could stay parked awhile. Here, we can leave the dogs inside while we're gone."

He helped her put the salad and beverages back in the refrigerator, then followed her out to the car.

A deluge of memories hit him when he slid into the front passenger side door. "Whoa."

She gave him a knowing glance as she turned on the ignition. "Miss this?"

He sat silently for a minute. "I didn't think I ever would. But just climbing in gave me that old surge of excitement. The longing for a hot call. A big case. Something really challenging. Exciting. Dangerous, even."

"I know. It hits me every single day. The hardest days are when I have to end up at a desk."

They drove in companionable silence, the

empty, black velvet ribbon of highway melting beneath the tires. She pulled up at the E.R. and frowned as several staff hurried past her front bumper. “This is the night entrance. It’s usually quiet out here this time of night unless a patient comes in, but—”

Several others came out of the hospital and hurried in another direction. She stared after them as she got out of the car. “You can come in or wait. Your call.”

An older nurse appeared at the glass doors. She squinted out into the darkness, then came running out to Megan’s door. “He’s gone. Oh, my—I don’t know how it happened—but Carl Wilson is gone.”

Megan stepped out of the car to face her. “He passed away?”

“No—no—he’s gone. And it’s as if he vanished into thin air.”

THIRTEEN

Scott followed as Megan hurried down the hall of the E.R., past the four exam rooms to the handful of rooms allocated to the hospital.

She was firing questions at the nurse as she strode through the E.R. "Have you checked every room, Bonnie? Under beds? The storerooms and closets? Maybe he awoke and became confused."

"We've gone through the entire hospital, yes," the nurse said breathlessly as she trotted to keep up with Megan's long strides. "And now we're searching the grounds. We called the sheriff's department just a few minutes ago. You sure got here fast."

"I was already on my way. Carl's daughter called me and said she was worried about her father." She pulled to a stop at the open doorway of Carl's room, then looked over her shoulder at the nurse and nodded toward Scott. "This is Scott Anders. He lives outside of town now, though he's on leave from a police department in the Chicago area."

Bonnie looked at him with new respect, sparing him a quick, strained smile before turning back to Megan. "It's unbelievable that Mr. Wilson could be gone. He wasn't even conscious, far as we knew. He hadn't spoken a word, nor opened his eyes. We'd checked in on him ten…maybe fifteen minutes earlier to changes his IV line."

"How many people are on duty right now?"

"No one's been brought into the E.R. tonight, so the E.R. nurse and I both cover the hospital side, plus the skilled and long-term beds. We call in more help if things get busy. We also have two nurse's aides, plus a housekeeper."

"No receptionist?"

"She leaves at eight-thirty, when visiting hours are over. The calls just route to the nurse's station after that."

Megan glanced at her watch. "Then

she left about a half hour ago. Before Carl disappeared?"

Bonnie nodded, her face pale and tight with worry. "We usually have a security guy who doubles up as an orderly when need be, because the place is so small. But he went home with the stomach flu early in the evening."

"So where were all the staff members during that time frame?"

"Paula—the other nurse—and I were changing a catheter on one of the skilled patients down the other hall. Ed can be combative, so it takes two and it's still quite a battle sometimes. The aides were on the long-term unit helping everyone get ready for bed. The housekeeper was on break."

"What about the doors?"

"Everything is locked at eight-thirty. You can exit but not enter—except the E.R. entrance."

"Alarms?"

"Always on down the long-term hallway. Automatically set everywhere else at eight-thirty, though on all of those, you can touch a button set high on the door frame that will let you out. And if someone goes through the

E.R. entrance, we hear a bell and they are caught on the security camera—like the one at the front door. We've got TV monitors at both nurse's stations."

"So a weak, confused man technically couldn't leave the building without setting off an alarm."

Bonnie nodded.

"Carl's daughter called me to say that a stranger was spotted in the vicinity of his room earlier."

"That's right. He isn't allowed visitors, period. Paula saw someone at his doorway. When she hurried down the hallway to stop him from going in, the man just took off." Bonnie shook her head in disgust. "We've had that happen before, though...someone coming in as a visitor, then scouting rooms for needles and meds as if we'd be careless to leave any of that stuff lying around. One day, someone even stole some purses."

At a commotion behind them, Scott turned and saw three deputies at the E.R. entrance talking to an agitated woman in a nurse's uniform.

"Wait here," Megan said to him as she went to join them.

He watched her speak to them, feeling an unexpected sense of pride in her professional demeanor as she clearly took command of the situation. Then two of the deputies went back outside and the taller, older of the three followed her up to Carl's room.

She quickly introduced Scott to the deputy, Jim Rigby. "Wes and Ewan are organizing a search outside and are alerting the dispatcher. Jim and I want to search the hospital. Scott can come with me. Okay?"

The nurse nodded. "I just hope we can find Carl soon. He must be very weak—he hasn't been on his feet since the accident."

"Can we play back those security tapes?" Jim asked.

"I...I think so. They feed into both nurse's stations, but the main unit is in the security office." She pulled a heavy key ring from her pocket and fumbled through it. "I'll go let you in."

"And I'm going to search Carl's room."

Scott watched from the doorway as Megan meticulously searched the room Carl had been in. “You’d be a good homicide investigator,” he said quietly.

“With the limited size of our sheriff’s department, we have to do everything. You just never know what the next day will bring.” She smiled briefly. “I’m sure this is the complete opposite of the extensive staffing and specialization you’re used to.”

He thought of the turmoil back in that Chicago suburb. His traitorous former partner, and the two fellow cops who had resisted his determination to uncover the truth. Proving they’d all been involved in a complex drug scheme had been the death knell of his ability to work in that precinct. “It wasn’t…what you might expect.”

She gave the room a last glance. “I don’t see anything here. No signs of struggle. Nothing out of place. It’s as if he simply got up and checked out after a nice nap…or someone kidnapped him. But how easy would it be to get past the staff and cameras, lugging a grown man?”

“Not very.”

“I’m going to search the hospital wing. Want to help?”

"Absolutely."

"Sorry about your dinner. By the time we get done here, the salad will be limp, and the entrée will be petrified."

"I know it would've been wonderful. The next time around it'll be my turn. Maybe I can take you out to dinner? I've heard the Cove is right on the water, and it's supposed to be excellent."

Her green eyes sparkled. "I'd like that."

He felt an inordinate amount of pleasure at her response. "Good. So, lead the way, Officer. Let's get this guy found and back to bed where he belongs."

An hour later, every room, every closet and the hospital grounds had been thoroughly searched.

Four patrol cars slowly, methodically cruised through town for hours after that.

But there wasn't a single sign that Carl Wilson had ever existed.

Sunday dawned with lightning spearing through the roiling clouds overhead, and heavy thunder that shook the earth. Rain slashed at the windows, rattling the panes. After being out late last night, leaving the delicious warmth of her down comforter had taken a concerted effort.

But now, walking up the wide steps of the Community Church amidst a sea of brightly colored umbrellas, she was thankful she'd made it. With her varying twelve-hour shifts, it wasn't always possible to attend.

As always, a sense of deep peace drifted through her as she stepped inside the old church with its towering white steeple and beautiful, burnished woodwork.

Pastor Fields stood just inside the door, greeting everyone with a hug or a handshake and a beaming smile, helping with raincoats and umbrellas as his flock came in one by one and stamped the rain from their feet.

"Megan." He smiled warmly, his white hair in cheerful contrast to his rosy cheeks. "*Wonderful* to see you on this beautiful day."

"It is a beautiful day. I love the rain."

He leaned closer and winked. "There's a young man here this morning...he arrived just a few minutes ago. I believe I've seen you with him in town."

To Pastor Fields, anyone under the age of

sixty was a young man, and he was forever playing genial matchmaker for his flock. Happily married for over fifty years, he was certain he was going to find the perfect young man for her. She smiled back. "I'll be sure to look for him."

She made her way through the people she'd known since she'd moved here, exchanging handshakes and hugs, and all of the usual pleasantries over sweet babies and engagement rings and news of children coming home from college, that marked the fabric of the community.

Someone brushed against her arm from behind as he passed. "Good morning." The voice was low, raspy, without any note of welcome.

She jerked to a stop and turned, but behind her she saw only a cluster of children and a couple of young moms framed by their umbrellas. But over there—at the edge of the parking lot, she caught a man giving her a quick glance before his black umbrella dropped back into place.

There was something vaguely familiar about his voice and profile…but who was he?

She watched him saunter away.

You've got to stop imagining things, she muttered to herself. *The poor man probably just has laryngitis, and you know half the people in this town at any rate. Of course you think you know him.*

And the last thing she wanted to think about right now was her job.

She slipped through the heavy oak inner doors into the hushed silence of the sanctuary and felt a sense of peace enfold her like welcoming arms.

It was a simple country church with a single center aisle and old-fashioned oak pews that marched up to the communion railing in front of the altar.

The walls at either side were white, set with twelve tall, old-fashioned and intricate stained glass windows depicting the events of Jesus's life. On sunny days, bejeweled light streamed through them in glorious colors. On this rainy morning they were dark and dreary, but with even greater meaning for all that Jesus had suffered in His time on earth.

She moved forward and settled in her favorite pew, three rows from the back, nodding to the others who had already come in.

The entire front of the church, including the altar, pulpit and lectern were oak, darkened to a deep, rich glow by the past hundred years, and generations of women armed with soft cloth and lemon oil polish.

She loved the honey and amber glow of the wood. The simple cross that hung above the altar with such deep meaning for her eternal life and the God who had been with her through good times and bad, her rock no matter what. *Lord, thank You for this beautiful day, and for all of the people here. Please, help me in the coming week to do my best for them. And please, please be with Carl and his daughter as we continue to search for him.*

Someone touched her shoulder and she automatically gathered her purse and jacket, then slid down the pew to make room. Her heart did that funny little dance again when she realized it was Scott.

"Good morning," she whispered. "You're up early."

"Attila thinks he's a rooster," he whispered

back in a low tone. "He announces dawn with the most unbelievable racket."

"I'll bet he's just the cutest thing, braying like that."

Scott slid his hand over hers and gave it a gentle squeeze. "Hey, I don't suppose I could interest you in a donkey."

A warm sensation shimmered up her arm at the touch of his hand, and it took a moment for her to collect her thoughts. "Um…a donkey. That sounds like a *great* idea. My nights are pretty short as it is, but thanks, anyway."

The organist began to play a soft, slow version of "How Great Thou Art," and Megan settled back in the pew, savoring the warmth of Scott's hand on hers. Missing it, when he shifted and pulled a hymnal from the pew rack in front of them.

He'd talked about no longer having trust that God would take the time to answer his prayers or watch out for him, but here he was anyhow, joining in a community of believers. She hadn't been so faithful back when Laura died.

At a time when she'd needed to be surrounded by a congregation of people who cared and who were shell-shocked and grieving, too, she'd pulled away, refusing to go to church or even talk to God in prayer for years afterward.

She shook herself out of her thoughts, startled when she realized that Pastor Fields was already at the pulpit.

"Send forth your light and your truth, let them guide me," he intoned, his voice deep and powerful. "'Let me bring peace to your holy mountains, to the place where you dwell.'" That's from Psalms 43:3, and I think it's the perfect verse for today.

"Many of us are fearful these days, knowing that evil is among us. Someone who has taken lives, and who has still eluded capture. Some question why bad things can happen to good people. Where is God in all of this? Why doesn't He intervene—and send a bolt of lightning to stop the one who can so callously take lives? Isn't He powerful enough to do that?"

A nervous titter spread through the congregation, and several people shifted in their pews.

"God gave us all free will, to do good or

evil. We're not puppets on a string. Evil does happen. I believe God sorrows deeply when His children go astray. He wants us to have full, happy, abundant lives in Him. And He is with us, wanting to give us strength and wisdom, and guidance. He is only a prayer away…"

Megan closed her eyes, the image of Carl Wilson taking over her thoughts. Where was he? How could such an ill man just disappear? Unless…

Her eyes flew open. He'd said he could identify the driver of the pickup truck…and Arnold Lane was missing. Had Lane snuck back into town, to hide in the hospital until visiting hours were over?

She'd watched the security camera tapes over and over, and there hadn't been even a hint of activity or the sounding of an alarm at the doors closest to Carl's room—the most logical route for a weak, confused man to wander away without being seen in the corridors of the hospital. There'd been no shred of evidence that anyone else had helped him leave. Hal and Jim had discounted the idea already, based on the tapes.

But it was possible.

Arnold was a burly man. Could he have hidden somewhere to wait until the staff was preoccupied, then dragged Wilson to a nearby side door? Disabled the alarm, and timed his exit to miss the sweep of that surveillance camera and avoid being seen? If so, he'd been able to disappear into the night with the one witness who could identify him.

And with the note left on the Fairlands' door, it seemed logical that Lane had not only caused the semi accident, but was also the Full Moon Killer.

She started to rise in her seat.

Scott gently took her hand and tugged her back down with a look of concern. "Are you all right?" he whispered.

"Yes—no—" She looked up and saw Pastor Fields was still giving his sermon, though his eyes were on her. The faintest of smiles touched his mouth, along with a slight cant of his head toward the door. "Pastor will understand. I need to leave."

She slipped past Scott and quietly left the sanctuary of the church, then she raced for her car.

They'd all been looking in the wrong place.

Carl Wilson wasn't in town. He probably wasn't even alive. But the search needed to widen or there'd be no chance at all of finding the one person who had seen the Full Moon Killer's face.

FOURTEEN

Since it was Sunday and her day off, she'd driven her own truck to church. She climbed inside and grabbed her cell phone from the console. Hesitated, then called Hal's private number. She hadn't seen him in church, but maybe he was at home with his ill wife.

He answered on the fourth ring. "Megan. What's up?"

"You know that Carl Wilson is missing."

"Jim called me last night and said the guy wandered off. Any news? Wait—this is your day off. Where are you?"

"In the church parking lot."

"Then you're running mighty late."

"I was there, and I left. I don't think Carl wandered off. He couldn't have. I still think he was kidnapped."

There was a long silence. "Why do you think that?"

"Just consider what we know. He wasn't even verbal, and he was flat in bed. The hospital staff thinks he woke up, got confused and wandered away. Maybe that's possible, but with all of the security cameras and door alarms, it would have taken a miracle for him to avoid both the staff and cameras, *and* disarm the doors."

"True."

"And why would he want to do that, anyway?"

"Confusion?"

"I just don't buy it. But he sure would be a valuable commodity to someone. He's the one person who can identify the driver of the other vehicle in his accident—a man who appears to be tied to the Full Moon killings. And now, coincidentally, Arnold Lane has come up missing. A suspect."

"Go on."

"Lane could've read all about the accident and Carl in the local newspaper. Realized that he had an opportunity to get rid of the man who'd seen his face. He could've slipped into the hospital undetected during visiting hours, then dragged Carl out. He could've decided to kill him and hide the body, or maybe dumped him in some remote area, figuring the guy would die anyway without care and there'd still be the question of whether or not Carl had escaped the hospital on his own."

"Sounds more than plausible to me. Hold on." Hal came back on the phone a few seconds later and sighed. "Looks to me like Jim and Wes got called in for overtime four hours last night, and now they're back on the day shift as scheduled. This isn't good. It just isn't good."

"True. But we're managing."

"You should talk Anders into coming on board on a permanent basis, Meg. He's got experience. Big-city stuff. He could be a real asset."

"He's already said he's not interested." She thought for a moment. "Maybe he'd agree to ongoing work on a consultant basis, but he said he wouldn't consider anything more."

"Still…"

"And you know the county wouldn't approve another full-time position, anyway. It's just a matter of getting our regular guys back on the schedule…unless someone decides to quit or retire."

As Hal wanted to do.

What would it be like to take his place, and have Scott working under her…or vice versa? Interesting thought.

"It's my day off, but I don't want to take it. Give it to me later." She turned on the ignition of her truck and threw it into gear. "I'll go out to my place and switch vehicles, and I'll call dispatch on the way. Everyone needs to be on the lookout for Carl, county wide."

"I'll be in a little later, too." Hal heaved another sigh. "And in the meantime, I'll be praying that circling vultures don't lead us to him. We need his testimony because right now it's all we got."

With the highway patrol and sheriff's department on alert, there were more officers searching. But in a mountainous area like Marshall County, it still didn't amount to much. Now and then the bodies of hikers missing several years or more turned up, and those accidental deaths weren't even intentionally hidden.

So the chances of finding Carl Wilson's body—if it had been buried in a well-hidden place—were roughly zero.

Still, every available officer joined in the search. On Wednesday, twenty volunteers on the search and rescue team came in with horses and dogs, and began scouring the country around Copper Cliff.

The dogs all hit on a scent from the side door of the hospital to the alley behind the hospital, but there the scent ended. So Carl had been put in a vehicle—but what then?

The team members fanned out, covered old timber roads and trails in a five-mile radius, then ten. Thirty more riders came from the neighboring county with horses and dogs, riding along highways and into government land.

The second day passed. A third.

And then the call came in from a man covering the Eagle Butte area five miles west of town. Megan arrived just minutes before the rescue squad and EMTs.

A man stood by the side of the gravel road holding the reins of a buckskin mare, his search and rescue dog leashed at his side. “I’m not sure about this one,” he said slowly, his voice grim. “I’ve got a body down there, but it looks like it’s been there awhile, and it’s been in the sun. It may or may not be the guy you’re looking for.”

Megan nodded, already rehearsing the difficult words she would have to say to Carl Wilson’s daughter. “Where is it?”

He pointed to the bottom of a deep, rocky ravine. “Be careful. It’s a tricky climb down, and I had some trouble getting out of there on the way back up.”

Even from up here she could smell the unique, nauseating stench of a human cadaver. “Can you wait here and flag down the emergency vehicles when they arrive?”

“Of course.”

She studied the steep slope, then started down at an angle, loose rock giving way under her feet and careening to the bottom way below. Halfway down, she could make out a leg protruding from a clump of sagebrush.

But as she drew closer, something wasn’t right.

Carl Wilson was around five-foot-nine.

Stocky—probably around one-ninety, or so. This body was much bigger, and it wasn't just due to the bloating of decomposition.

She reached the bottom, scanned the area for hazards, then held a tissue at her nose as she walked up to the body for a closer look. She did a double take.

The guy was dead, all right. Someone had made sure of that.

The body was sprawled like a rag doll on the rocks, the shirt torn away by its long, rocky trip down into the ravine. She could see two bullet wounds in his chest.

But it wasn't the condition of the body that made her take a second look. It was the identity of the victim.

This wasn't the truck driver.

It was Arnold Lane, and someone had wanted to make very, *very* sure he died.

Which meant Carl Wilson was still missing.

The real killer was still out there.

And if he stayed true to his pattern, there were just eleven days left before he'd strike again.

* * *

Megan pulled into her drive at eight-thirty and wearily climbed out of her patrol car.

It had been a long, long day.

Arnold Lane had been positively identified, and that eliminated their most likely suspect. But was his death related, or had he simply ticked off one too many people with his charming personality?

Hal and Jim were investigating his activities during his absences from the ranch but had come up dry so far, and that left far too many unanswered questions.

She whistled for Buddy and waited to hear the dog door slap shut at the back of the house, and for Buddy to come barreling around the side of the house to clamber at the gate of the chain-link fence as he always did, begging for attention. With every passing day, he seemed brighter, stronger and more alert, acting more and more like a pup than an old dog in his joy over his new home.

But the little door didn't slap shut.

No dog appeared.

"Buddy?"

An uneasy feeling crawled through her as

she let herself into the yard and walked around the house. Where was he?

Inside, her footsteps echoed in the empty house. Even before she walked through every room, she sensed that she was completely alone. If the dog had died, she was going to be heartbroken. *"Oh, Buddy,"* she whispered. "Where are you?"

But he simply wasn't here. The yard gate had been securely fastened. And she knew he wasn't agile enough to leap the fence, which left only the possibility of theft. But who would steal a dog?

Mystified, she looked through the two bedrooms once more, checking under beds and in the corners. And then she saw a folded piece of paper tucked under a fat sandalwood candle on the dresser.

She lifted the candle, carefully opened the piece of paper by its edges, and despite all of her years in law enforcement, her heart caught in her throat.

Bang. You're dead.
You could've been, if you were here.

Sorry I missed you—but there will be another time. I promise you that.

Anger rushed through her as she read the note, then read it a second time. Someone had been here. In her house. Violating her personal space. What if she'd been asleep and hadn't heard him break into the house?

She could defend herself in hand-to-hand combat. Packed a gun and shot better than ninety-eight percent on her marksmanship tests every quarter. But she was still vulnerable—as anyone was.

And the mere presence of this note made that message perfectly clear.

FIFTEEN

Scott called an hour later and said he was stopping by. Calling ahead was a wise decision. If he hadn't, she would've had her service revolver loaded and ready at the first sound of a vehicle coming up the lane.

She met him out in the driveway. "What's up?"

"You sounded tense on the phone just now," he said, hooking his elbow in the open window of his truck and draping his other hand over the top of the steering wheel. Next to him, Jasper watched her expectantly, his tongue lolling and his tail thumping on the seat. "I've been worried about you since you took off during church on Sunday. Is everything all right?"

"Not the best. I told Hal that he needed to

hire you permanently, because we definitely need more help."

"Did you also tell him that I'm not interested?"

"Nope." She grinned. "I figured we could work on that little detail later. Hal is such a nice guy that it can be very hard to say no."

Scott shifted in his seat and glanced behind her, then gave her a quizzical look. "Is that a gun at the small of your back?"

She'd left her T-shirt untucked to better mask her lower-back holster, but he certainly had a good eye for detail. "Could be."

His eyes flashed with instant curiosity. "Really?"

She snorted. "And you say you have no interest in being a cop."

"I don't. So what is it?"

"My backup weapon. Glock 23, 9mm."

"Nice. So what's going on?"

Despite her initial reservations about working with him, she'd come to trust him and his sharp perceptions. Compared to working with Wes or Ewan, his thoughtful analysis of details was a complete breath of fresh air. "This week's newspaper will be running a story on the body found in the ravine. We're probably going to see the panic level rise around here… and start receiving a lot more calls concerning possible tips."

He nodded.

She considered her words carefully. "When Carl Wilson disappeared from his hospital bed, it seemed possible that he could've been kidnapped by Arnold Lane, our prime suspect in the serial killings."

"True. If Lane drove that black pickup and caused Carl's accident, he might've feared that Carl could identify him."

"It just got more complicated than that. A search-and-rescue dog found Lane's body this morning. He'd been murdered and dumped in a ravine."

Scott thought for a minute. "Obviously a very ill, older man like Carl couldn't have done it."

"Not a chance."

"So you've got someone else out there… someone with a vested interest in getting Lane out of the way." Scott frowned as he stepped out of his truck, closed the door and leaned against it. "Someone who may or may not be tied to the serial murders."

"Exactly." She glanced over her shoulder at the house.

He followed her gaze. "Where's your dog? Is he all right?"

Scott wasn't part of the sheriff's department. He hadn't been around long enough to build the kind of unshakable trust between them that could grow only over years of shared experiences.

And yet her gut instinct told her that if she was ever in serious trouble out here, he'd be a powerful ally. And it didn't take much thought to realize that he'd be the one she should call first.

"Buddy was missing when I got home. I searched everywhere and ultimately found him chained inside the barn."

"Something you never do?"

"Of course not. He can let himself in and out of the house through a dog door, and he has a locked, fenced yard. So someone was here while I was gone."

"Kind of coincidental, isn't it—with everything that's been happening?" Scott's words were light, but his eyes were dark with concern.

She sighed. "It's no coincidence. Someone wanted to deliver a message, to remind me that I'm vulnerable. It isn't the first time it's happened. And in case I didn't understand the implied message, he left a note."

A muscle at the side of Scott's jaw ticked. "This evening."

"Yep."

"Have you called the sheriff's office?"

"I *work* there. I don't need to call for another deputy to come out and tell me what I already know."

"Which is?"

"An unidentified man broke into my house. He terrified my dog—Buddy was shaking when I found him. The font style on the note matched the one I received before—and also matches a note carried by a victim that our rapist/serial killer set free. For some reason, this animal has targeted me personally. He's daring me to catch him. But we aren't closer to doing that than we were a month ago."

"Arnold Lane's death does seem to eliminate a suspect."

"But we still don't have any solid leads… other than the fact that the guy seems to have a laser printer and likes using pretty fonts when he writes me threatening notes."

"And he has a particular interest in you. Which makes me think that once upon a time you either jilted him, arrested him, or did something to make him really mad."

"I have no past boyfriends with wounded hearts, believe me. My two most serious relationships ended because the guys couldn't deal with my career. I haven't dated at all in a good long while."

"What about enemies? Investment deals… arguments over land…legal suits…"

"This place was on the market for over two years before I bought it. The owners were relieved to finally make the sale. And with my salary and the mortgage on this place, I'm hardly looking into any investment schemes."

"Any particularly nasty arrests?"

"Of course. A few. Not many people are happy when they end up with a hefty speeding ticket, or in jail, or prison. The domestic situations are the worst. But I've never had any revenge threats that I can think of." She smiled a little, remembering a few. "Well, maybe by some drunks, but I'd bet they didn't remember a word they said by the next day."

"Any other ideas why someone would target you?"

"I've read a lot of studies. Some said that most rapists feel deep hostility toward women, so they take pleasure in physical coercion. It makes them feel like real 'he-men,' because they aren't anything close." She snorted in disgust. "I'm guessing the suspect is toying with me because I'm a woman and a cop—two figures he hates. If he can make me afraid, he'll feel like a *really* tough guy. The ultimate power trip."

"You can't stay out here alone. Not anymore."

"What? I should run and give him that satisfaction? No way."

"Megan—"

"It isn't going to happen."

"Look at your house."

"What?"

"Take a good look, because that old wood siding won't stop a bullet. With the right ammo—available anywhere—your friend could blast holes through those walls until all you had left was matchsticks, and you would be dead. If this guy is after you, you won't be safe here."

"I'm well aware of that. But I have a dog. I'm well armed."

"Do you have friends in town?" He paced a few yards away, then turned back. "Any place else you can go? One of the other deputies, maybe?"

"No. If I did that, I'd only draw danger there. And honestly, I don't think this guy plans anything like that. He's getting his thrills with innocent victims. From me, he's getting the pleasure of proving himself invincible and uncatchable." She paused. "If that's even a word."

"But he *will* escalate."

"I think we're going to get him first."

"There are no guarantees of that, Megan. Come to my place, then—at least until this is all over. I've got a lot more room there than I'll ever use."

"Now, that would look appropriate," she

said, trying for a light tone. "What would my mother say?"

"Does it matter, if your life is at stake?" He thought for a moment. "Then how about this. There's only one, dead-end lane leading up to my property. Anyone coming up there would have to go right past my house, dog and Terminator."

"Who?"

"That goose I bought at the auction. He goes after everything that walks, crawls or slithers and he's even noisier than the donkey. He has the mailman terrified, so no one else will get past him, either."

She managed a smile. "What a sweetie."

"Look, there's also a stone guest cottage a few hundred feet back of the house, with water and electricity. You could use it as long as you need to."

She gently pulled her hand from his. "I still don't—"

"Consider it a safe house. The previous owners were going to use it as a mother-in-law's place, so it's pretty nice."

"It's really thoughtful of you to offer. I do

appreciate it. But…I can't accept. I need to stay right where I am."

He stared at her. "You really don't understand how serious this is. I don't care if you're armed to the teeth—it would take just a single bullet for you to die. You aren't safe here. You don't need to take that kind of risk."

Spoken just like her last boyfriend, who'd ordered her to give up her job and her independence, and play it safe with some ordinary job in town.

Her old hurt and frustration resurfaced. She'd thought Scott was different, that he'd understand her life. But instead, he knew the dangers all too well, and now she knew that he'd never be able to stand by and let her face them.

Once again she'd started to care too deeply about someone, and she'd been wrong.

"I know you don't want to be a cop any longer. If you can't handle it anymore, that's okay. But this is my life, and I can. I *need* to do my job. End of story."

He pulled back as if she'd struck him. "I didn't mean to interfere." He hesitated, then shook his head with obvious regret as he got back into his truck. "Have it your way. But don't hesitate to call me if you ever need help."

His words sounded so final that she knew he wouldn't be back, even if she did try to make that call. She watched him drive away, feeling a cold, unfamiliar knot build in her stomach.

Most men assumed she was eminently capable of taking care of herself. But Scott was a guardian at heart—whether he'd left his old career behind or not—and he'd been trying his best to protect her.

Unfortunately, he was right.

Dusk was settling in, turning the landscape to shades of indigo, violet and ash. In another hour it would be black as pitch. Anyone could creep up in the dark and start firing....

And the house would be a much easier target than some lone gunman slipping through the trees.

SIXTEEN

After a sleepless night of pacing, and startling at every rustle of leaves outside, Megan took a quick shower, dressed and took Buddy out to her patrol car. "You're coming with me today. No sense taking any chances."

She looked over the open car door at the house she'd loved from the first moment she saw it, wondering if she'd ever feel truly safe there again.

Today she'd make some phone calls about security systems, but she had no misconceptions about that being a fail-safe plan. As Scott had said, a gunman could shoot the place to pieces, shattering windows and doors. A hail of random bullets could take down someone inside.

Or the guy could gain access himself, day or night, catch her unaware and be gone before the alarm system ever brought lights and sirens to her door. How long could she go on, trying to sleep with a loaded gun under her pillow and her ears attuned to every sound?

Buddy curled up on the passenger side of the front seat, his eyes fixed on her profile as if he, too, was wary of unknown dangers that might take away his safe world in a heartbeat.

She reached over to stroke his soft ears as she headed down the highway to Copper Cliff. "We'll be fine, Buddy. You'll see."

But *fine* was a relative thing, and her conversation with Scott last night now started playing through her thoughts for the hundredth time. He had that innate need to protect, but as a deputy she did, too. With such similarities, how had things gone so suddenly wrong? Maybe if they could just talk it through…

Two miles out of town her cell rang. Her heart rose on a burst of joy and she grabbed the phone from her pocket without glancing at the screen. "Scott. Everything was fine at the house last night."

"Really. How *very* nice to hear."

She froze at the all-too-familiar, sinuous voice. "Who is this?"

"Sweetheart, I thought you'd guess by now. So sad…when I've shared clues with you, just to see if you were worthy." His voice rang with arrogance and smug pride. "But you're not."

"*What* clues? A couple of notes?" She fought to keep her voice calm as she struggled to identify the muffled voice. She *knew* it. She'd heard it before—but where? She scrambled for something to ask, anything to keep him talking. "I…I'm curious. Why did you choose me? Why not one of the other deputies? Or the sheriff himself?"

Buddy whined and edged closer to rest his head on her lap as if he sensed her tension.

"You see, that was your first clue, the best one of all. You disappoint me, Megan."

Megan.

It was the odd, soft way he said it. A stray wisp of memory floated out of the past, then slipped just out of reach. She knew him somehow. Even with the muffling of that voice, she *knew* him.

"I was going to wait. My timetable, you know. I rather enjoyed seeing you people trying to figure it out. But now I'm bored and I think I'll up the stakes."

"Stakes? I don't understand. Tell me what you mean."

"I think it might be you who's next. Maybe one of those good friends of yours. Who are they? Let's see...Erin and Kris come to mind."

Her heartbeat tripled, making her suddenly feel faint. "There's no reason to harm anyone. Not anymore."

"Actually, there is."

"Look—you've fooled us all. You were smarter than everyone, so you're still free. If... if you just stop now, no one will ever catch you. Wouldn't that be the best thing? To never face Montana's death penalty?"

"I'm not concerned about that." His voice grew harsh. "But you could stop it, you know. It was always all about you."

She blinked, her blood turning to ice at the implication. "I...I don't understand."

"You will. I'll call again soon. Maybe tonight, maybe next week. When you're alone, like you are right now. What is it like, Megan, to feel fear taking over your heart? To not know what will happen next?"

The connection went dead.

She slammed on the brakes and twisted in her seat to look back. The highway behind her was empty. *So how did he know she was alone?*

Had he been back at the house, watching her leave?

Or had he tailed her, then slipped off into a side road before she'd notice?

With trembling fingers she speed-dialed Erin, then Kris, to warn them, urging them to either stay behind locked doors or leave town until they heard from her again.

Kris had her animal rescue shelter to run. Erin said she couldn't possibly leave her store at the start of tourist season. But though both promised to be careful, Megan's heart filled with dread. *Please, God—watch over my friends. Keep them in Your safe and loving care. And please, please let me find that killer first, before it's too late.*

At the sheriff's office Megan strode past Betty's desk without stopping and went straight to Hal's office with Buddy close at her heels.

The door was locked.

She wheeled back and stopped at the

startled secretary's desk. "Where is he? Is he in there?"

"Gracious! He's out working Jim's shift today, dear. He's been gone for a good hour or more."

"I need to talk to him."

"You can use the radio...but if this is something important, you'd better call his cell."

Megan headed for the deputy's office and shut the door behind her. Hal answered after a couple rings.

"Megan—good. This saves me a call later. We got a report from someone up here near Fuller Peak, so Ewan and I went. Carl Wilson has been found."

She closed her eyes and said a swift, silent prayer. "Is he dead?"

"Would've been, if some hikers hadn't found him when they did. He just had a thin shirt and those cotton hospital pants on. He looks dehydrated and he's delirious. With these cold nights up here and the fever he's got, he probably has pneumonia on top of everything else."

"He couldn't have gotten up there on his own. No way."

"Someone saw a dark-colored truck go up the fire road over the weekend—but they don't remember which day. It looks like Wilson was dumped up here and left to die. It's an absolute miracle that he was found."

"Is he talking at all?"

"Yeah, but he's not making any sense. The EMTs think he'll come around once they get the IV started so they can get him rehydrated."

Please, God, let that be true. "So he might be able to identify the man he saw on the highway."

"We can hope. But with all he's been through, I just don't know…or if his testimony would even hold up in court, if it comes to that."

"I've got other news you need to hear. I've heard from that caller again. He says he's going to 'move up his schedule,' and he named his potential targets. Erin Cole in Lost Falls. Kris Donaldson in Battle Creek. Or me."

Hal didn't speak for a minute. "Those other two women are in Latimer County. His targets have only been here. Maybe this one isn't really our man."

"It is," she said flatly. "I have no doubt. It's the same voice. The women he named are childhood friends of mine."

"How would he know that?"

"We're all still close. He could've seen us together. Or…" A face from the past materialized in her thoughts. A faint memory of an encounter on the Main Street of Lost Falls. And suddenly she *knew* that face, though the name still escaped her. "I'll call you back. I need to go home and get something—something important."

"Wait—"

"I have an idea, but I need to see something first. If I'm right, we might be able to get this guy off the streets before it's too late for anyone else."

The drive home usually took twenty minutes, but now she floored the accelerator on the straight, empty stretch of highway.

The caller had sounded vaguely familiar, his voice muffled and roughened with age. And then there'd been that man at church—the one who'd brushed past her. She'd caught just a brief glimpse of him, and again, there'd been something oddly familiar—like seeing a face through the other side of a tropical fish tank, the water blurring the lines and planes until the similarity between image and reality was too vague to judge.

But there'd been yet another encounter, and now all the pieces were starting to come together. If she was right, the results were chilling.

The Full Moon Killer had been at the Half-way House Tavern the night she was there. He'd been in Lost Falls all the time she'd been there as a child. And his vendetta went back that far, too.

Just what kind of man had he become? A ruthless killer—or someone too sick to even comprehend or care about what he was doing?

She lifted her mike. Debated about calling backup, then changed her mind. Everyone else was stretched to the limit with overtime, barely able to cover the county as it was.

It was broad daylight, and the caller had taunted her about calling back another time.

So surely he wasn't waiting at her cabin now.

At home she sat in her patrol for several minutes, watching the house and surrounding terrain before unlocking the safety on her Glock.

Buddy bounded out of the car when she stepped outside and ran ahead of her to the yard gate, his tail wagging. When she opened the gate, he raced around the corner to the back of the house, where she heard the familiar slap of the pet door opening and shutting.

In a flash, she saw him at a front window, his paws on the sill and his nose pressed to the glass while he waited for her to come in. "That's sure a good sign," she said aloud as she unlocked the front door and walked inside. "Am I ever thankful for you."

Still, she took care to lock the door behind her, and she took note of everything in the room before going any farther. It was all untouched, as far as she could tell.

Buddy joyously nuzzled her hand, then jumped up on his favorite end of the sofa, circled twice and flopped down, though he still watched her intently as she crossed the room to the spare bedroom.

The closet was crammed nearly to the ceiling with boxes she'd never bothered to unpack. Holstering her gun, she started lifting them out one by one, reading labels and setting them aside. Her impatience grew, along with her worry. Hadn't she kept that single box of mementoes from childhood and high school?

Had it been lost during one of her many moves from one apartment to the next?

She checked each of them again. Searched under the bed. Then went to her bedroom and checked that closet, as well. No dice.

Closing her eyes, she thought back through the years. Then she speed-dialed Erin and prayed that her old friend had been more sentimental about the past.

"Megan?" Erin sounded breathless. "Is everything all right? Did you catch that guy?"

"No...not yet. But I need a favor. Do you still have your old high school yearbook?"

"My *yearbook?*"

"I can't find mine. I need some pages, as fast as I can get them. It's important."

"Goodness. I'm sure I have it somewhere... maybe in the attic. Can I look for it tomorrow? We were just going out, and—"

"If you've got it, I need it now. If you don't, I'll call Kris."

"Kris? You're kidding. I doubt she even bought one, with the way she had to move around so much in high school, poor thing."

"This is important, Erin."

Erin grew quiet. "Is this about your call earlier? About that man who's making those threats?"

"It is."

"Give me ten minutes. I'm going up to the attic right now. If it isn't there, it could be in some boxes I put in the storeroom over at the store. I won't leave home until I find it, I promise."

"When you do, I need you to copy and fax every page of the sophomore through senior pictures. You have that capability there at the store, right?"

"Sure do."

"Send it here—to my fax at home." Megan rattled off the number, then paced through the house waiting for the fax to ring.

Five minutes. Ten. Fifteen.

Buddy jumped off the couch and followed her, then stopped at the front door and whined, clawing at the door. "You've got your own door, Buddy. Go ahead."

He whined louder.

She moved to a window and pulled the curtain back a few inches to survey the yard.

"There's nothing out there. Do you smell a rabbit or something?"

The first bullet smashed through the window in front of her and sent searing pain through her right hand, spattering her shirt with blood. The second broke the neighboring window and whistled past her ear, sending glass shards slicing across her cheek. Crying out, she stumbled backward, trying to staunch the heavy flow of blood from her shattered hand with the hem of her shirt.

Buddy yelped and ran for the kitchen, his tail between his legs. She spun around and followed, putting another wall between her and the shooter, then grabbed for the phone above the counter.

The line was dead.

With her good hand she rummaged in a drawer for a kitchen towel and then wrapped it tightly around the wound. She tried to tighten her fist. Pain rocketed up her arm, sending dark spots in front of her eyes. He'd gotten her gun hand—possibly shattered bone. There was no way she could grip her weapon and shoot with accuracy. Left-handed, she'd never been able to do better than seventy percent accuracy on the range.

She searched her empty pockets for her cell. *Where was it?* She'd paced all through the house in her impatience. She'd had it her hand…

Another living room window exploded, followed by the lamp next to the sofa. Crouching low, she edged to the corner of the kitchen door. The ruby gleam of her cell phone taunted her from over by the front entrance. Too far. Too much risk. Yet if she didn't call for backup…

She turned, gauging the distance to the door. If she could make it across the yard and vault over the fence, then she could reach the surrounding forest. There were deer trails back there, some that ran close to the highway.

From outside she heard a twig snap, then another, coming around the side of the cabin. *Too late.*

Once again, a series of bullets shattered glass, this time at the back door and kitchen windows.

"Come on, Buddy. Where are you?" She scanned the room for the terrified dog. He'd disappeared, but with luck he'd sense her departure and run after her.

Another window shattered, this time by the kitchen table.

A prayer on her lips, she crouched low and ran for the front door, reached up to twist the dead bolt and glanced outside, then grabbed her cell phone from the floor and raced for the open front gate and her patrol car. Fifteen feet to go. Ten—

In front of her, the driver's side window shattered into tiny prisms of safety glass that bloomed inward like crystalline fabric with one perfect, round, nine-millimeter hole in the center.

"I don't think you'll be going anywhere just yet, Megan."

The voice was clear now, unfiltered by whatever he'd put over his phone receiver in the past. She turned slowly and looked into his almost familiar face.

A face that had aged; one that had been repaired and remolded over the years after the meth-lab explosion when he was just a teen. But it was still a face she'd sworn she'd never forget. *"Rex."*

Rex Nelson. Son of the former sheriff.

"Move nice and slow. Release the buckle of your service belt. Let it fall. Touch that weapon and I'll blow you apart."

She fumbled with the buckle, feigning a concerted effort.

"*Now,* or you lose a knee." He watched with intense fascination as her service belt hit the ground, and with it, her gun. "I've waited so long for this. I thought about it for years, behind bars. When I found out you were a deputy, I couldn't believe my luck. It's been fun, putting you to the test."

"Test?" Horrified, she stared at him. Had those other deaths been part of a plan that he'd been mounting against *her?*

"At first I just wanted to make you look stupid—for you to publicly fail. To lose your reputation and career." He fluttered his hand dismissively. "Perfect justice for what happened to my father. But obviously that didn't work, so now we need to move to Step Two."

"I…I don't understand."

"Don't toy with me—of course you do. You deserve to suffer as much as I have." His mouth twisted. "You and your cousin Erin purposely *destroyed* my family—and that friend of yours, too. And now I'm going to pay back each of you. One by one by one. But…I don't think you'll be the first to die. I believe I'll leave you here while I go see the other two. Then you can dwell on your sins while you bleed your life away."

He pulled a long, gleaming bowie knife from a leather scabbard at his side and ran a thumb along the edge. A thin red line welled up in its wake.

Time—she needed more time. "None of us tried to destroy your family. We were just kids back then. At least tell me what we did to deserve this."

"You remember the day my father and I left town. It was my senior year, and I didn't even get to finish it out. I saw you on the street and I yelled at you as we passed. Do you remember?"

She jerked her head in a single nod. "I couldn't make out the words."

"I said that I'd come back someday, and justice would be served." He bared his teeth in a smile. "And now it will be."

"But I did nothing to you. Ever."

His eyes narrowed, gleaming with a sudden rush of hatred that made her shudder. "Nothing? You all did nothing but complain, and vilify my father. Your whole family did, until they stirred up the whole town. He didn't mess up that murder investigation. He was a *good* sheriff. He did everything right. But you made sure he lost his job. And do you know what happened then?"

She shook her head, eyeing the blade as he took another step closer. She backed up another foot along the side of the car.

He was a good six feet of solid muscle. She was half his weight. Maybe she could take him down on a good day, but with only one good hand…

Could she move fast enough to get the gun out of her ankle holster? He was close. Too close. He'd be on her in a heartbeat if she tried. She thought of all the moves she'd learned in self-defense classes, considering and discarding one after another. His gun was trained on her chest, center mass. One wrong move and he could fire. *Lord, help me, here. I've got to warn Erin and Kris—I can't die here. Not right now.*

"My father drank himself to death. He lost his job, his pride, his future because of you. You see my face? A beating destroyed my nose in high school. One of his broken beer bottles finished the job after we left town." Rex's voice rose, dripping venom. "Each time I look in the mirror, I think of everything you did to destroy my father. And then I think of all the ways I'd like to see you die."

SEVENTEEN

Scott looked at the speedometer of his truck, then dropped down to seventy.

He'd been thinking about going back to Chicago before yesterday's argument with Megan. He'd known that he would have to go back sometime and deal with the trouble that was brewing in his absence.

He just hadn't planned on it right now.

But her words had struck him like a switchblade, and they'd been playing through his thoughts ever since. *I know you don't want to be a cop any longer. If you can't handle it anymore, that's okay.*

Is that what had happened? Had he chosen to use his medical leave as an escape, rather than to continue his fight against the corruption he'd found festering in the department?

Its roots were tangled deep into the very

fabric of the place he'd once loved so much, twisting among the men he'd once admired and some of the good cops he'd worked with on the street before moving into Homicide.

Once he'd started to delve into that sorry mess, he'd soon discovered that a bullet to the shoulder might not be the end of it, and he could end up paying with his life.

But now the airport was just a couple hours away. He had his bags packed, his tickets bought, and a neighbor was taking care of his animals.

So even though it was over with Megan—and she'd made that plenty clear—he could come back here with a clear conscience, after doing everything in his power to help clean up the problems in Chicago.

The cold, heavy weight taking the place of his heart expanded even more. *Megan.* From the moment he'd first seen her, he'd been entranced by her sparkling shamrock-green eyes and all of those golden highlights in her auburn hair.

And when she'd first started talking about her job—

He smiled to himself, remembering. She had the kind of fire he'd once had, before going out on one too many calls; seeing far too many gut-wrenching situations. He'd developed distance then, that protective shell that kept a guy from feeling too much.

But Megan—just being around her had made him feel alive again. Though the more he was with her, the more he feared for her… and that had swiftly led to the end of any hope for a future with a woman who had so totally captured his heart.

A woman who faced danger every day of her life, with courage and intelligence. Who was facing even greater danger now.

An uneasy feeling crept through him and wouldn't let go.

He looked at the speedometer again and realized he'd dropped to fifty. Then forty-five.

What was he thinking, leaving for Chicago now?

Maybe she'd insisted that she didn't need his help. Maybe she still wouldn't accept it. But if he didn't go back, he knew it would be a mistake.

And if the small, insistent voice of warning in his head was right, he might regret it for the rest of his life.

A wave of dizziness washed through her as Megan clamped her blood-soaked hand beneath her other arm, trying to stop the bleeding. *Keep him talking. Anything, to keep him here and find a way to stop him....*

"I...I thought you got those scars from that meth explosion in high school." Stars danced in front of her eyes as a wave of nausea rose through her midsection.

"Some, not that it matters anymore. And now I'm the one with all the power." Rex studied her, his mouth curved in smug satisfaction. He studied the gun in his right hand, the knife in his left. "It's so hard to choose. I almost hate to end this. But...I really should be going."

From the corner of her eye Megan saw Buddy cowering at the edge of the yard, a good thirty feet behind Rex. Even from here, she could see he was shaking with fear, though he didn't take his eyes off her face.

He was terrified of most men. She was sure he wouldn't dare come closer to this one. *Please, Buddy. Bark. Run. Anything for a distraction.*

He crept forward, his head and body lowered, his ears flat. *Come on, Buddy.*

With one fluid motion he coiled, then launched himself at Rex's back in a furious explosion of snapping jaws.

Rex fell forward with a scream, stumbling to his knees as he swung out with the side of his gun, smashing it against the side of Buddy's head. The dog yelped and fell motionless at his feet.

"Buddy!" Horror ripped through her, coupled with a surge of anger. She blinked and forced herself into the cool, methodical, professional persona born of thousands of hours of training over the years. She dropped to one knee to mask the motion of reaching for the small semiautomatic in her ankle holster.

"Oh, *please*." Sarcasm dripped from his voice as Rex stood up, two-handing his own gun. He raised it until she was looking down the barrel.

With a fierce cry she lunged forward, ramming her head into his stomach. He staggered backward, doubled over his arms. She spun, threw all her weight into her elbow and caught the side of his temple.

He sprawled on the ground, groaning…but when he rolled to one side he still had his gun held weakly in one trembling hand. A litany of curses flew from his mouth as he lifted it in her direction.

Out of the shadows another figure flew into view. *Scott.* Startled, Megan saw him dive for the gun, roll and jump to his feet, with the gun trained on Rex. "You won't be needing this, mister."

She immediately hurried to Buddy's side. The dog was lying flat and still where he'd fallen, a small pool of blood seeping from a jagged laceration at the side of his muzzle. "Oh, Buddy," she whispered, resting a gentle hand on his head and stroking his body. Joy exploded through her when she felt the faint, shallow rise and fall of his ribs. "He's breathing!"

At the sound of her voice, he lifted his head a few inches, then dropped back and managed a single thump of his tail.

She sat back on her heels and looked over at Scott. His face was pale and drawn, as if he were steeling himself against considerable pain radiating through his bad shoulder, and she knew what his swift action had cost him. But still, he was watching her with an expression so worried, so tender, that it nearly took her breath away. "You came back," she said in wonderment. "Why?"

"I had to," he said simply. "I couldn't walk away from the best thing I've ever found on this earth. I just hope you can forgive me."

She closed her eyes briefly, barely aware of the pain in her hand any longer as she tried to process the blessing standing before her—the answer to her desperate, silent prayers for help. "There's nothing to forgive, because you were right all along. It's me who should be sorry."

"I called 911 the minute I saw what was happening here, so they should arrive any minute. Why don't you call the vet and tell her that we'll be bringing Buddy in, and after the deputies haul away this guy, we can talk. Deal?"

Already she could hear the distant, discordant wail of sirens. At least three of them.

She nodded. "Believe me, there's nothing I want more."

* * *

Hal handcuffed Rex immediately, then he and Jim stuffed him in the backseat of one of the cruisers, where he had no chance of escape. It took nearly an hour more for the EMTs to examine and dress Megan's hand, and for Scott and Megan to finish answering questions.

"You need to get down to the hospital for X-rays," Scott said when they had left Buddy at the vet clinic for sutures and observation. "I can't imagine how much that hand hurts."

"It did, but now I guess it's sort of numb. All I can think about is how you appeared—perfect timing. Without you, I'd be dead right now, and Rex would be going after Kris and Erin. I can't tell you how hard I was praying."

"It looked to me like you were holding your own, despite everything," he said with a tender smile. He curved his arms around her in a gentle embrace, and lowered his mouth to hers for a quick kiss, and then one that was much, much longer. "I think I lost ten years of my life when I saw him going after you. The thought that he could have ended your life fills me with such…such anger, such a sense of loss, that I can't even fathom it."

"But now it's all over." She started to pull back, knowing that the high emotions of facing danger made people say things they wouldn't mean tomorrow. Since Scott had come into her life she'd discovered a hundred ways in which he seemed like the perfect man for her, but she knew he didn't feel the same. Not really. And sometimes, it was just better to cut your losses and run. "I guess we'd better get going."

He caught her uninjured wrist and gently pulled her back into his arms. "*Wait.* I once told you that I didn't think God was listening to me. I don't believe that anymore. I was driving to the airport when I had the worst sense that something was wrong. I knew I *had* to come back here, or I'd regret it forever. And the closer I got, the faster I drove, because I just knew that every second counted. I was praying every mile of the way that you'd be safe."

"Sometimes He answers us in different ways than we expect and in His own good time. Sometimes the answers aren't the ones we want." She felt her eyes burn. "But He brought you back to me, right when I needed you most."

"Tell me before we leave for the hospital, because if I have to wait much longer, I don't think my ole heart is going to make it. I know it's early days for asking this, but I just have to know. Do you think there's a chance for us? Despite everything?"

She smiled up at him, searching the depths of his eyes for what she'd hoped to find all her life. Acceptance. Understanding. And the tender beginnings of love. Her heart swelled until it seemed to fill her chest when she saw all of that and more—an echo of everything she was feeling, too.

"Absolutely." She wobbled on her tiptoes to give him a kiss, wishing the moment could last and last.

EPILOGUE

The warm Montana sunshine could be fickle up in the mountains, even in late July.

But now the late-afternoon sun sent a glittering array of diamonds dancing across the sapphire waves of Big Bear Lake, and a soft breeze through the towering trees filled the air with the sweet, sweet scent of pine. Fluffy white clouds rested in a robin's-egg-blue sky, at the tops of the mountain peaks to the west.

"No cathedral could be as beautiful as this," Megan murmured to Scott as they stood on a hill watching the people gathering at the lakeshore, where Erin and Jack would soon say their vows. Max, Jack's young nephew, stood near them, playing with his puppy Molly and Buddy, who had recovered from Rex's blow with only a scar.

Nearby, Trace stood with Kris, his arm around her shoulder as they talked to his sister Carrie, who had told everyone at the bridal dinner last night that she'd be moving away from her brother's ranch on Monday.

"Poor Kris," Megan murmured. "I know she and Carrie have become close as sisters. And now she's suddenly moving away."

"Did she say why? I thought she had a good job at the high school."

"That was the odd part—she wouldn't talk about it. She just insisted that the dinner was meant to be a night for happiness, and to let it go at that." Megan bit her lower lip. "It won't be easy for Kris to see her go…she's never given up on finding her sister Emma, and now this."

Scott gave her shoulders a gentle squeeze. "But things can work out, in God's good time. You taught me to have faith in that. So for today, let's just be happy for all the things that are good, okay?"

Megan stood on her tiptoes and brushed a kiss against his cheek. "You're absolutely right."

She still couldn't believe how well things had turned out after the Full Moon Killer has been brought to justice.

Hal had suffered a light heart attack the next day. He was doing just fine after surgery, but had decided it was the wake-up call he'd needed about finally taking the retirement he'd longed for. He'd be able to be with his wife all the time now, and both were happy sharing every day they had left.

Despite her long-standing reservations, Megan had agreed to step in as interim sheriff until the next election, and she was finding the job more rewarding than she'd expected. With the deputies all at work once again, the department was fully staffed, and Scott had finally made his trip back to Chicago.

It hadn't taken him long to uncover the truth—that the late drug dealer, Rico Mendez, had been involved with the crooked cops Scott had identified. To destroy Scott's credibility, he'd paid off a rookie cop to plant the ten grand in Scott's bank account and steal key evidence from the evidence room. Worse, he'd bribed the rookie to romance Scott's fiancée, trying to ferret out enough information about Scott to destroy him. The shallow woman had fallen for the guy in the process, though they'd both been fired and were facing charges.

Now that he was back in Montana after clearing his name, Scott seemed happier and more settled. He'd even agreed to a 50-percent position as a deputy, which would still give him time to write.

Better yet, he and Megan had been seeing each other every day, and each passing week had brought them closer.

Brimming with happiness, she clasped Scott's hand. "God's glory," she whispered, looking out at all of the friends and family assembled. "I see it in this beautiful place… and in all the love that's here today for Erin and Jack. It's all just so breathtaking—absolutely perfect."

"Not quite." He gently turned her around and rested his hands on her shoulders, locking his gaze on hers. "This day could be even more perfect."

She looked up at the depth of love in his

eyes and felt her heart warm and expand in her chest until she could barely breathe, too afraid to speak and risk shattering the moment.

He lowered his mouth to hers for a long, exquisite kiss that sent shivers through her and turned her knees weak.

"I hope you'll be my wife, Megan. If I could be with you until my last breath, I'd be the happiest man on earth. But think about it… don't answer until you're ready."

"Oh, Scott," she managed to say when she could at last catch her breath. "The answer is *yes*."

He kissed her again, and this time she kissed him back with all of the love in her heart, until she felt swept away toward a future she'd never imagined possible.

Only the gentle notes of a harp and violin duet at the water's edge broke their embrace. "Guess it's time to go," she whispered.

Thank You, Lord, for everything that happened today—for everything that turned out so right. A sense of peace drifted through her...as if He had just blessed the two of them with a promise of forever afters.

And with her heart overflowing with joy, she let Scott lead her down the hill to the waiting crowd.

* * * * *

Dear Reader,

I hope you've enjoyed your visit to the Montana Rockies in *End Game*, the third book of my BIG SKY SECRETS series. I have loved exploring the ways the three young heroines of these stories have dealt with the tragedy that occurred while they were growing up—how it changed them, how they overcame their emotional wounds, and along the way, how they found deeper faith. I hope you'll join me again later for two more Love Inspired Suspense novels in this series—Emma's story and Carrie's story. But before that, *Winter Reunion* will be out in November 2010, for the Love Inspired line.

All of us have encountered difficult times in life, and sometimes it's so hard to go on—to find peace, to find a way to forgive ourselves and others. I have found such comfort and support in the following verses, which are among my favorites...and perhaps you will, too!

> Don't worry about anything. Instead, pray about everything. Tell God what

you need, and thank him for all he has done. If you do this, you will experience God's peace, which is far more wonderful than the human mind can understand. His peace will guard your hearts and minds as you live in Jesus Christ.
—Philippians 4: 6–7

I love to hear from readers at P.O. Box 2550, Cedar Rapids, Iowa 52403. If you are online, you can visit my Web site at www.roxannerustand.com, e-mail me at rrustand@mchsi.com, or even better, visit my blog, "All Creatures Great and Small" at http: //roxannerustand.blogspot.com, a place where readers and authors exchange humorous and poignant stories about their animals.

Wishing you many blessings.

Roxanne

QUESTIONS FOR DISCUSSION

1. Megan Peters was driven to a career in law enforcement by a tragedy that occurred when she was young. Did situations in your own youth shape your own career choices as an adult?

2. In *Fatal Burn*, the second book in this series, Kris establishes an animal shelter, and in *End Game*, Megan adopts one of the older dogs at that shelter. Have you ever adopted a homeless animal?

3. Megan is absolutely focused on her goal in life: to capture criminals who victimize women. In looking at your own life, have you had a long-term goal or desire that has influenced your life?

4. Who was your favorite character in the book, and why?

5. Megan has long since given up on finding a happy, permanent romantic relationship, while Scott has been hurt recently by an

unfaithful fiancée. How do you think those past experiences will affect the romance between Megan and Scott? What will it take for them to have a happy, solid relationship that can last for a lifetime or is that possible?

6. Megan is a believer, and in her personal life would never frequent seedy taverns and flirt with the men in them, but does this in an effort to try to find the killer before he strikes again. Have you ever had to do something that was against your personal values, in order to help someone?

7. Scott comes back, at the end of the story, because he senses that something is wrong and is worried about Megan—and he is right. How does God answer our prayers? Would this be an example of a way in which God answers prayers, or not?

8. Which person in your life would you call on if you were in trouble, and why?

9. Who did you think was the murderer? Were you surprised when his true identity was revealed?

10. Scott is a believer, yet he has lost his confidence about God's love and concern for him in his daily life. What evidence of God's caring do you see in your own life and how your prayers are answered?

11. Scott's engagement ended when his fiancée abruptly ran off with someone else, leaving him certain that he didn't want to risk his heart again. Have you ever had a romantic heartbreak? What were your feelings about it, and how long did it take you to heal? How do you feel about that person now?

12. The next book in this series will involve Emma, Kris Donaldson's sister, who has been missing for many years after leading a troubled life as a teenager. Has there ever been a falling-out between you and another family member? Was it possible for everyone to forgive and forget, and become completely accepting?